DESPERATE MEN

Deputy Sheriff Matt Cameron was worried as he rode back to town after unsuccessfully hunting rustlers. Lawlessness was on the increase, and Matt had heard that his brother Buck was riding with Eli Kimber's gang. He had warned Buck off years earlier and his brother had dropped out of sight. Now it seemed Buck was back on the crooked trail. Matt also had a showdown looming in the shape of Hulk Grayson, the bullying town slaughterman. Trouble piled up when he found Ben Turner, the liveryman, murdered, and when he caught up with Buck. Now it would all flare into deadly action.

DESPERATE MEN

DESPERATE MEN

by

Corba Sunman

Dales Large Print Books
Long Preston, North Yorkshire,
BD23 4ND, England.

British Library Cataloguing in Publication Data.

Sunman, Corba
    Desperate men.

    A catalogue record of this book is
    available from the British Library

    ISBN   978-1-84262-717-4 pbk

First published in Great Britain in 2008 by Robert Hale Limited

Cover illustration © Gordon Crabb by arrangement with
Alison Eldred

Published in Large Print 2009 by arrangement with
Robert Hale Ltd

Dales Large Print is an imprint of Library Magna Books Ltd.

Printed and bound in Great Britain by
T.J. (International) Ltd., Cornwall, PL28 8RW

ONE

Matt Cameron sent his black up the muddy slope and, when he reached the crest, the pelting rain hit him full in the face despite the low brim of his Stetson. Spring in Montana, he thought grimly, was no place for the faint-hearted. He reined up and glanced at the grey sky which showed no signs of relaxing the downpour. Great grey-black clouds, full-bellied with unshed water, were being harried across the sky by the unrelenting wind, as if the good Lord had ordered a heavenly round-up. He could hear the muttering sounds of the river in the background as he twisted in his saddle to glance back over the sage and juniper slopes on his back trail. He suspected that he had been followed covertly ever since he left Dan Benton's cattle ranch – B Bar – where he had investigated a report that a herd of prime steers had gone missing from the home pasture.

The deputy sheriff star on Matt's slicker was dull in the wet. He had seen his fiancée,

Ginny Benton, out at B Bar, and she told him she thought she had caught a glimpse of his brother Buck early that morning skulking in the brush near the ranch house; a report which Matt discounted because he had told Buck he would kill him if he ever clapped eyes on him again, and for three years there had been no sign of his no-good brother.

Ginny taught the local kids in the new schoolhouse on the edge of Buffalo Crossing, and when they married in late summer as planned, it had been arranged that Matt would turn in his law badge, take over the running of the B Bar ranch and settle down to family life. He was looking forward to marriage and the changes it would inevitably bring, but the fear that Buck Cameron might turn up again did nothing for his peace of mind. Buck, who had always lived dangerously on the edge of lawlessness, was bad news in any man's language.

A peal of thunder rolled and echoed through the grey overhead mass and reverberated in the surrounding hills. The rain suddenly increased – great spikes of it hammering the already sodden ground and sweeping across the landscape under the never-ending harassment of the cold wind.

Aware that he would not see anyone unless the rain eased, Matt sent the black on again, heading for the blurred outlines of the huddled buildings just ahead that housed the 300-strong community of Buffalo Crossing. His thoughts were sombre. Someone had stolen a herd from B Bar and he had been unable to find any trace of the thieves.

Lately there had been a spate of lawlessness in the county – small stuff that did not amount to much, mere pinpricks in the fabric of lawful existence, but they were warnings that a bad element was growing, and the suspicion that his brother Buck might have moved back into the area gave Matt serious food for thought. The last man he wanted to see at this time was Buck.

The main street of Buffalo Crossing was awash with puddles and the hoofs of his black splashed through them as Matt rode to the sidewalk in front of the law office. He tucked his chin deeper into the upturned collar of his slicker as he dismounted and wrapped his reins around the hitch rail. His searching glance around the deserted street saw nothing suspicious and he heaved a sigh of relief as he stamped his boots on the sidewalk and thrust open the door of the office.

Sheriff Tom Flynn was seated at his desk,

chin in his hands, head nodding and eyes closed, lulled by the steady, soothing roar of the rain hammering against the sloping roof. Water was splashing into a bucket set in a corner, having found its way through a loose shingle overhead. Flynn reared up when Cameron slammed the street door, and the old sheriff rubbed his eyes and leaned back in his seat, his pale-blue eyes blinking owlishly as he fought against sleep. His long, weathered face, with its wrinkled forehead fringed with iron-grey hair, looked pale, unwell. Matt paused to subject his superior to a keen glance of appraisal, aware that Flynn had been feeling ill for weeks.

'How did you make out at B Bar, Matt?' Flynn demanded.

'They had a herd taken out of their home pasture.' Matt grimaced. 'There were twenty steers in a prime herd and the thieves had the audacity to ride right in there and steal them. I think we've got bad trouble coming, Tom. I looked around some out there, but it was too wet to do the job properly and I'll have to go back when the rain eases. There are a couple of nester families by Antelope Creek and it's likely they know something about the steers. How are you feeling? You ain't looking too good.'

'I ain't well at all.' Flynn tottered to his feet and stood with his hands pressed on the desk, his head hanging forward. 'I've been waiting for you to get back so I can go home to bed down for a spell. I saw the doc this morning and he gave me some more physic but it ain't doing me any damn good. You'll be all right on your own, huh? The town is quiet. If I have an early night I might feel better in the morning.'

'Sure. You get along right now. I'll stable my horse, get something to eat, and then stick around here.' Tall and broad-shouldered, Matt was all muscle and whip-cord with a reputation of never having been beaten in a fist-fight. He was better than average in the use of the .45 pistol in the cutaway holster thronged down on his right thigh, and was well thought of in the county.

'Lock the office whenever you leave it, Matt.' Flynn took a slicker from a hook on the back of the street door and pulled it around his shoulders. 'I've made up my mind to quit this job when you get married. I reckon I can last out till then, but when you leave they'll need two new lawmen around here.'

The sheriff departed and Matt stood lost in thought for some moments. Tom Flynn had been the sheriff of Watson County for nearly thirty years and his name was legend. He had brought peace to an untamed land and, with his ability and tireless efforts, had maintained the letter of the law since before Matt was born. The end of an era was approaching, and Matt could only admire the older man's impeccable record.

Matt stifled a sigh of regret and locked the office door when he departed. The evening was throwing shadows into the corners now, the rain continuing unabated. Lights were beginning to show in some of the buildings fronting the street, but not many folks were venturing out in the bad weather. He swung into his saddle and rode along the street to the livery stable, which was gloomy in the murk. He dismounted just inside the building. Rain was slapping relentlessly against the roof and he could hear the drip, drip, drip of water leaking through it in several places.

'Hey, Ben, ain't it about time you gave us some light?' he called, and his voice echoed through the shadows. He waited, listening intently. A horse stamped inside the barn but there was no response from Ben Turner, the ostler, and Matt stepped down from his saddle, trailed his reins and crossed to the small office in a corner where Turner spent most of his life. 'Are you asleep, Ben?' he demanded.

He paused in the doorway of the office, produced a match and struck it, then moved to the lantern on the desk. When the lamp flared he turned up the wick and stared down at Ben Turner, who was seated in his chair with his back to the door, his upper body slumped across the desk positioned against the far wall.

'Ben, are you all right?' he demanded.

His teeth clicked together in shock when he spotted a trickle of blood on the desk under Turner's head. He felt for a pulse and found no throb of life. Turner was dead, his body rigid and cold.

Matt stood motionless, his eyes recording the scene instinctively. He saw splotches of blood between Turner's shoulder blades, and the shape of the six thin stab wounds in the back of the man's coat indicated that he had been stabbed repeatedly. Matt drew a sharp breath and straightened. Turner had been murdered by someone who had found the liveryman an easy mark sitting with his back to the door.

He left the stable at a run and hurried along the street to the house of Doc Crickmore. There was a light in the front window and the doctor came to the door in response to Matt's heavy fist pounding on the centre panel. Crickmore was in his fifties, a tall, thin man who had administered to the sick of the county for more than twenty years.

'What's the trouble? Is it the sheriff?' Crickmore demanded.

'No, it is Ben Turner. He's dead in his office at the stable,' Matt spoke breathlessly. 'He's been stabbed in the back. You'd better come, Doc.'

Crickmore smothered an imprecation and turned to snatch up his medical bag. Matt led the way back to the stable, and stood in the doorway of the office while the doctor entered to examine the body. A loose board somewhere at the rear of the stable was banging monotonously under the relentless force of the never-ending wind, and rain dripped ceaselessly through the weak spots in the roof.

'He's been dead maybe three hours,' Crickmore said at length. 'He was stabbed six times, and never had a chance to defend himself. Have you got any idea who might have done this, Matt?'

'It looks like the work of a maniac,' Matt replied, shaking his head. He approached

14

the desk and stood behind the chair. A metal cash box, open and empty, was on the desk. 'Ben always had a pile of greenbacks in that box, so it looks like robbery is the motive.' He glanced around the office and observed, 'There's no sign of a knife, and whoever did this will probably have blood on his clothes. I'd better get around town and see what I can turn up.'

'So who would take a knife to Ben when a blunt instrument would have been more practical?' Crickmore grimaced. 'As you say this looks like a madman's work. Ben was a good man and didn't have an enemy in the world. Are there any strangers in town? I can't believe one of the residents could do something like this, not even for money.'

'I take your point,' Matt mused. 'I can't imagine anyone who knew Ben doing it. I've been out on the range all day and just got back so I don't know who is in town. You finish off here, Doc, and get Tom Piercey to take care of the body while I scout around.'

Matt lighted a lantern and carried it to his horse, which was standing patiently with trailing reins where he had left it. He took care of the animal, his movements instinctive; his brain whirling in shock at his grim discovery. This was cold-blooded murder, and the theft of stock from the B Bar ranch faded in comparison.

When Matt went back to the door of the little office, Crickmore was ready to leave. The doctor picked up his medical bag.

'That's all I can do here, Matt. I'll get Piercey to remove the body to his establishment and then I'd better inform Betty Turner her husband is dead. That poor woman hasn't been well for months, and bad news like this could kill her.'

Matt nodded. He was feeling out of his depth, and made an effort to get a grip on his thoughts.

'I'll check the town for strangers,' he said, and turned swiftly away from the office. His brain seemed to be on fire and shock was coursing strongly through his veins. Ben Turner had been callously murdered and robbed! The knowledge throbbed through his head with maddening insistence. There was a motive for the murder, but no suspects.

He walked around the barn with the lantern held high, looking for a horse that might belong to a stranger, but he knew every animal by sight and hung the lantern on a nail in a post just inside the front door before going out to the street.

16

The general store was ablaze with yellow light and Matt entered to find Will Carmody, the storekeeper, serving a woman. Carmody, slightly built and short in stature, was chatting animatedly with Bella Grayson, the town butcher's wife, and they were laughing together in a light-hearted fashion. Carmody looked up, still smiling, and lifted a friendly hand.

'Be right with you, Matt,' he called.

Bella Grayson, in her middle forties, was tall with a well-developed figure. She wore her blonde hair long, had a more than passably attractive face, and always showed a keen interest in Matt whenever they met around town. She never missed an opportunity to touch him – sometimes a tug at his neckerchief or a show of picking a non-existent thread off his clothes – actions which disconcerted him because he was only too aware that her husband Hulk Grayson was an over-jealous man by nature and had caused trouble in the past by taking offence at the way some of the townsmen looked at his wife. Now she glanced at Matt and half-smiled, but her expression seemed strained, and he felt a pang of relief because for once she appeared to want to remain at a distance.

'I just want to know if you've seen any strangers around town today, Will,' Matt said.

'No, I can't say as I have.' Carmody shook his greying head. 'How's the sheriff. I haven't seen him today. Is he still feeling ill?'

'He went home to bed when I got back from B Bar.' Matt was watching Bella Grayson's expressive face and saw her mouth pull into a thin line. She took up her purchases and turned hurriedly for the door, avoiding his eyes, her head averted.

'It's getting late,' she observed. 'I'd better get home or Hulk will be in for his meal before it is ready.' She glanced at Matt, signalled expressively with her eyes, and then lowered her head and hurried out of the store.

'What have you done to her?' Carmody demanded, grinning. 'She's usually a lot friendlier with you. Do you reckon Hulk has warned her off? She seemed to have taken a shine to you, and you could get odds around town that Hulk would tackle you before the month is out. That star you're wearing has probably stayed his hand. He'd face a long spell behind bars if he lost his temper again, especially with you.'

'She seems upset about something,' Matt

replied. 'Are you sure you haven't seen any strangers around?'

'Positive. This day has been real busy. I've been run off my feet from the moment I opened up this morning and I'm glad it's about time to close. Sorry I can't help you, Matt. I shall be glad to sit down and put my feet up. Is there anything you want before I close?'

'Nothing!' Matt turned to the door and departed, intending to visit the two saloons along the street. He pulled his chin deeper into the collar of his slicker and suppressed a shiver as a spatter of rain splashed into his face. He needed a hot meal but there seemed little likelihood of appeasing his hunger in the near future. He paused on the sidewalk and looked around at the shadows before moving on.

A hand grasped his right arm as he passed the darkened premises of the local gun shop and he halted abruptly, his hands lifting, but stayed his instinctive response when Bella Grayson spoke in a husky whisper.

'Matt, please help me!' Her voice sounded shaky with emotion. 'I'm so worried about Hulk. I'm afraid he's going to get himself into trouble with the law.'

'What makes you say that, Bella? Who is

he picking on now? I thought I'd made it clear to him the last time he stepped out of line that if he hurt anyone again he'd get a jail sentence.'

'It's not that! I'm sure he's learned his lesson as far as that is concerned. I've threatened to leave him if he hits anyone else and he knows I would do it. No! He's got thick with Jack Tarmy and those two hard-cases he hangs around with, and I think he's going to take some rustled steers from them. Can you do something about that without making it official? I wouldn't want Hulk to go to jail. Can you give him a good talking to and warn him off? Or if you caught Tarny and his pards rustling stock and jailed them it would take temptation out of Hulk's way. Tarmy is a real bad man, but Hulk isn't.'

'That's a serious allegation, Bella,' Matt said. 'Have you any proof that Hulk is getting mixed up in that kind of trade?'

'I heard him talking with Tarmy. He said he is willing to take a couple of steers a week if the price is right, but they haven't gone beyond the point of talking about it yet. Please do something, Matt, or there will be bad trouble around here if they do start rustling. Hulk is bull-headed and won't

20

listen to anything I say. You've got to nip this in the bud, Matt.'

'Leave it with me, Bella. Don't worry about a thing. I'll get round to Hulk before long, and I'll keep it unofficial.'

He started to move away but Bella reached out and grasped his arm.

'Thank you, Matt. I knew I could rely on you. I'll appreciate anything you can do.'

Matt heaved a sigh as Bella turned and hurried away. He went on to Brants Saloon and pushed through the batwings to pause on the threshold. A dozen men were present in the big room, and Matt looked them over, noting that they were all residents. He crossed to the bar and called to Jack Ryder, the bar tender, who came along the bar with the ease of long experience.

'What can I get you, Matt?' Ryder was a small man with an easy manner and a ready smile. He looked a lot younger than his fifty years. His sparse brown hair was slicked down and he wore a well-trimmed moustache that curved above his top lip.

'Nothing to drink right now, Jack,' Matt replied. 'I haven't eaten yet and I'm empty as a drum. I might drop in again later, if I can find the time. I just want to know if you've seen any strangers around today.'

Ryder shook his head. 'Nary a one,' he replied cheerfully. 'Is something wrong? You look kind of strained, Matt. Is the job getting you down? I can't understand why a young feller like you is tied up in the law business. You're at everyone's beck and call, and a target for any galoot who fancies his chances against you. What made you take a star in the first place?'

'I haven't got time to chat, Jack, but one of these day I'll bend your ear a little and explain my motives. Are you sure you haven't seen any strangers?'

'The place has been like a graveyard.' Ryder shook his head. 'It's the rain. It keeps everyone off the street. I haven't even seen the sheriff today, and he usually drops in for a tot of his favourite medicine.'

Matt thought of Ben Turner lying dead in the livery barn and compressed his lips. Ben's killer had not been deterred by the rain.

'Tom went home to bed when I got back from B Bar,' he said. 'He ain't been feeling well today. I think there's a lot more wrong with him than he admits to.'

Matt left the saloon and walked to Mike's Bar, half a block away. The bar was smaller than Brant's Saloon, and only three men

22

were inside when Matt entered. Mike Gibson, the owner, was standing behind the short bar, and nodded when Matt approached him, his dark eyes glinting in the lamp light. He was a tall, thin man of few words, with hollow cheeks and a forbidding expression. He wore a dark-blue store suit and looked like an undertaker with his unsmiling face.

'Have you seen any strangers around today, Mike?' Matt asked.

'No.' Gibson's face did not change expression.

Matt waited for more of an answer but Gibson remained silent.

'Well, thanks for that mine of information!' Matt shrugged resignedly, turned and left the establishment to stand on the sidewalk for a moment gazing around the rain-swept street while considering his next move.

He walked along the shadowed street towards the sheriff's house, his thoughts returning to what Bella had told him. Hulk Grayson was prepared to buy two rustled steers a week on the cheap and it came to him that B Bar had lost stock from their home pasture the previous night. He paused while he considered the fact and, on an impulse, crossed the street to go to Hulk Grayson's slaughterhouse on the back lots behind the bank, hoping that he was not too late to put a stop to Hulk's plan before it got under way.

He entered the alley beside the darkened bank, and was halfway along the alley when he heard a furtive sound at his back and swung around. A shadow was close behind him, and he was dimly aware of movement. He grasped the butt of his gun but a heavy object crashed against his hat and a brilliant flash seemed to explode inside his skull. Then blackness encompassed him and he fell forward on to his face and lost consciousness.

TWO

Matt regained his senses to find his face pressed into the mud of the alley. Rain was pelting down on his body. He lifted a hand to his head, discovered a painful swelling just above his right ear, and pushed himself to his hands and knees and waited for his senses to stop gyrating. At first he could not recall what had happened. His mind was blank and he figured he was having some kind of a nightmare. Then his memory returned and he thrust himself upright and leaned against the wall of the bank.

Someone had slugged him! Matt was shocked by the events building up in his mind – Ben Turner murdered, Bella Grayson informing against her husband, and now he had been attacked right here in town. What the hell was going on?

He reached for his pistol, found the holster empty, and dropped to his knees to feel around for the weapon. He froze when a harsh voice spoke from the surrounding shadows.

'I've got your gun, Matt. I wanta talk to you, and this is the safe way to do it.'

Matt looked up. A tall figure was before him, barely visible against the backdrop of shadows, but reflected lamp light gleamed on the barrel of a pistol that was pointing at him. His mind whirled as he recognized the voice: his brother Buck! He leaned back against the bank wall for support.

'Ginny said she thought she saw you skulking around B Bar,' Matt said.

'I was hanging around out there because I wanted her to give you a message, but she didn't come out of the house to see me. Then you showed up so I followed you back to town. I need to talk to you, Matt.'

'I don't want to hear anything you've got to say.' Matt pressed a hand to his aching head. 'I told you three years ago that I'd shoot you if I ever clapped eyes on you again, and nothing has changed, Buck. You're poison as far as I'm concerned! What the hell do you want? Can't you stay away from honest folks? You chose your way of life a long time ago and you'll have to stick to it. If I ever get the chance to put you behind bars then I'll do it without a second thought.'

'I know all about that,' Buck Cameron spoke harshly. 'We've had our differences in the past, Matt, but you better hear me out. I'm risking my life to warn you of a bad business that's coming up here, and the least you can do is listen to what I've got to say.'

'I never knew you to tell the truth about anything, so why should I believe you now? I wouldn't accept anything you said, so you're wasting your time. What are you up to? I couldn't trust you any further than I could throw you with one hand tied behind my back. I thought I'd seen the last of you after that trouble you got into over in Ridgeville, but you keep turning up like a bad penny. Why don't you leave me alone?'

'Listen, Matt. You've got big trouble coming your way. Let's go somewhere private so I can fill you in on it.'

'I don't want to be in your company a minute longer than I have to be. What's on your mind, Buck? Make it quick. I got a lot on my plate right now.'

'If you're talking about the liveryman being murdered then I know about it,' Buck said. 'He was killed as a warning to you that they mean business, and there'll be others dead around here tomorrow if you don't go along with what I've got in mind.'

'Are you serious? What do you know about Ben Turner's death? Who killed him?' Matt stifled a groan as his brain whirled. 'Buck, you've pulled some bad tricks in your time, but I never knew you to get involved in murder. I hope you had nothing to do with Turner's death because I'll put a rope around your neck if I find you're involved.'

'I didn't do it. Now are you gonna listen to me or do I leave you to face the trouble alone? If you don't do like I say then a lot of people will surely get killed.'

'Stop talking in riddles and tell me what's on your mind,' Matt said harshly.

'Let's go along to your office and talk. We're being watched right now, and if you try to get the better of me you'll take a slug in the back. You've got nothing to lose by listening to me. The men I'm working with are real bad killers. I wish I'd never set eyes on them, but they've got me like a fish on a hook and they would kill me if they knew I was planning to double-cross them.'

'That sounds more like you,' Matt observed. 'They're too tough for you, is that it? And the only way you can get rid of them is by turning them over to the law. What are you after – the price on their heads?'

'That comes into it,' Buck chuckled harshly. 'If I can pick up the bounty offered for them you'll never see me again, not in this life. I'll be off to South America. But first I've got to take care of Eli Kimber and his crooked bunch. There's only one way a man can quit Kimber's gang and that's with a bullet in his back. Well, I reckon to turn that around and cold-deck them.'

'And get the law to help you.' Matt shook his head. 'I don't want to get mixed up with that bunch.'

'You don't have a choice. Kimber plans to get hold of Ginny and some of the school kids tomorrow morning and hold them hostage until his gang has cleaned out the bank. If he doesn't get any trouble from the townsfolk then he'll turn his hostages loose soon as he's clear of the town.'

Matt caught his breath. 'Are you on the level, Buck?' he demanded.

'Why else would I be here trying to convince you? Hell I wouldn't dream of playing games with Kimber. I do draw the line at murder, but that gang is real brutal. They don't care how many folk get killed so long as they get what they want, and right now the bank in this town is their target. Kimber has planned this down to the last detail. The town has been under observation for weeks now. They know the sheriff is ill and you're on your own. Ben Turner was knifed this afternoon as a start to the raid, to show you they mean business, and unless you toe the line and stay clear of town tomorrow there will be a lot more bloodshed.'

'Let's go along to my office,' Matt said sharply. 'I guess I have to take you at your word. If you're on the level then I'd be a fool not to listen to you. But if I find you're trying to run a sandy on me I'll throw you in a cell and lose the key.'

'This is too serious for me to try any tricks, Matt. You're really up against it. There are six men in the Kimber gang, and they are all killers. Crazy Joe Stott came into town this afternoon and knifed Ben Turner. He's the worst of the bunch, but not by much – Wiley Brunt and Gus Pank run him a close second. They try to outdo each other when it comes to murder.'

Matt led the way back to the street and headed for the law office. He could think of no reason why Buck would want to trick him, and the situation was too desperate for him to take any kind of a chance with the safety of the community, who relied on him to uphold the law, but he would have no chance alone against six of the toughest criminals who ever rode the back trails of the West.

Buck followed him silently. Matt unlocked the office door and entered to light the lamp on the desk. Buck followed him inside and closed the door. Matt turned to face his brother. They were much alike physically. Buck was the younger by two years, but looked ten years older than Matt's twenty-four. His way of life was apparently taking a heavy toll. His face was drawn and his dark eyes held a glitter which Matt had not seen before.

'Is that my gun you're holding?' Matt demanded. Buck grinned sheepishly and placed the weapon on a corner of the desk.

'Sorry I had to smack you on the head,' he said, 'but I couldn't take any chances with you. Listen, Matt. You haven't got much time left. The gang will he moving into town early in the morning. What Kimber wants is you out of here until the gang have got their hands on the bank dough.'

'I can have a dozen townsmen ready and armed in here inside of twenty minutes,' Matt said. 'You know me well enough to realize that I can't pull out and leave the town wide open to a bunch of desperadoes.'

'Kimber already has two hostages. He stopped off at a nester place on Antelope Creek and grabbed Frank Wenn and his wife. If you try to fort up in town and resist Kimber the Wenns will be the first to get it, and tomorrow Kimber will have Ginny and some of the school kids in his hands. He plans to have the kids with the gang when they go into the bank, and any shooting at them will surely hit those kids. You've got to ride out, Matt, and Kimber wants to see you go. One of the gang is outside now, watching you. If you try to organize resistance you'll take a slug in the back. You'd better listen to me, and don't make any mistakes. One wrong move will be your last, and with you dead the whole town will be at Kimber's mercy.'

'There's more to this than you're telling me,' Matt mused. 'I know you too well, Buck. What's behind all this rigmarole? I know about the Kimber gang, and they wouldn't set up something like this. They'd just ride in and start shooting at everyone who stood against them, including me. So why don't you level with me and tell the truth?'

'OK.' Buck sighed and shook his head. 'I'll give it to you straight. When Kimber came up with the plan to raid the bank in town I mentioned you were a deputy here and I wouldn't want you to get hurt. Kimber said for me to get you out of town while the raid took place, and this scheme is the best I could think of.'

'I don't like the bit about taking hostages.' Matt shook his head. 'But if I do ride out as Kimber wants, how do you put the gang in a corner?'

'I'll tell you where the gang will be hiding out after the robbery. But you've got to ride out of town tonight. When you're in the clear you can make for B Bar, but hold your hand until Ginny has left the ranch for town. When she's gone you can go to Dan Benton, tell him what's happening, and I'll lay a dollar to a plugged nickel he will put his outfit at your disposal to get Ginny back.'

'I could ride out to the ranch now and warn Ginny against going to the school in the morning.'

'You'd never make it. Jesse Coe is out there watching, and if you show up at the ranch before Ginny leaves then Coe will put you down in the dust.'

Matt considered Buck's words. He was of a mind to stand and fight not run, but with innocent people at risk he knew he could not take any chances.

'Where will the gang hide out after the raid?' he asked.

'Now you're talking!' Buck grinned. 'There's a hideout in the hills west of Greenville. It's a great place because the gang can watch the approaches and have plenty of time to get away if a posse should show up because there's a gully at the rear by which they can escape. So you can bring a posse to block that bolt-hole and trap them. Send some men in at the front and get the gang when they make a run for it out back.'

'I can't trust you, Buck.' Matt gazed into his brother's eyes and Buck grinned sheepishly. 'You've pulled some bad tricks in your time. Just what are you up to now?'

'All I know is that you don't have a choice, Matt. I'm bending over backwards to give you a chance of staying alive and putting Kimber's bunch out of action. You've got to think of the hostages. Already there's a man and his wife being held, and tomorrow Ginny and some of the school kids will be grabbed. I know what that gang is capable of, and if you know anything at all about them then you won't have to think twice about what you should do. You can't get to Ginny and warn her off so go along with what I've worked out and you could come out on top where it matters most. Anything short of what I suggest will end in disaster

34

for this town.'

'Where's the exact location of the hideout the gang will make for after the raid?' Matt asked.

'It is north of Antelope Creek. Follow the game trail into the hills. There is a dead tree where the trail splits in two. Follow the trail north in the direction of Broken Horn and when you cross the first big ridge in that direction you head west into the hills. There's a rock big as a church lying on the range that looks like it shouldn't be there – there are no other rocks around for miles. A game trail leads up into the hills and you follow that until you hit broken country. The trail goes through a gully and there are a couple of caves near the top end. That's where the gang will be.'

'And how do I get to the bolt-hole?' Matt demanded.

'Don't go into the gully where the cave is. Stay out of it and circle right. You'll need to leave your horses about then and climb up a bluff. Walk ahead and if you're not careful you'll fall into the gully where the bolt-hole is. I reckon you'll need a twenty-man posse to take the gang because they are real desperate men and they won't surrender.'

Matt was racked by indecision. He wished

the sheriff was well enough to handle this deal because so many things could go wrong. But was Buck telling the truth? He doubted he could take his brother's word with so much at stake. But if hostages had already been taken then their lives would be forfeit if he did not do as Kimber wanted.

'It's a tough choice, Matt,' Buck observed. 'I wouldn't want to be in your boots and have to make a decision. But you have to think of the hostages. Do it like Kimber says and no one will get hurt.'

'I'd rather trust a snake than a man like Kimber.' Matt shook his head. 'There's no way I can go along with what you're suggesting. Someone in town might spot the raid in progress and start shooting.'

'You can't cover for every possible angle. When the townsmen see hostages with the gang I reckon they'll hold their fire.'

Matt sat down behind the sheriff's desk and opened a drawer to take out a sheaf of wanted posters. He scanned through them, looking at rough drawings of hard-faced thieves and killers. He found Eli Kimber's sullen face and gazed at it, failing to see any sign of human compassion in its stark lines. A pair of screwed-up merciless eyes peered out of the poster from under thick eyebrows seemingly clinging to a protruding forehead. A mass of unkempt black hair covered a large skull and a straggly beard concealed most of the cheeks and prominent chin.

'He looks like a cave-man,' Matt observed.

'And acts like one,' Buck countered. 'There's no way you can reason with him. Do as he says or take the consequences.'

'Look through these dodgers and pick out the rest of the gang, if they are among them,' Matt said.

Buck rifled through the sheaf, and selected five other posters from the pile. He flicked them in front of Matt, who scanned them for details.

'Crazy Joe Stott,' he read aloud. 'Six feet tall; fair-haired; carries a knife and a gun – a wanton killer to be approached with great caution.'

'He's the worst of the bunch after Kimber,' Buck picked up the third poster. 'This one is nearly as bad – Wiley Brunt. He loves killing people.'

Matt gazed at the grim countenance on the poster. There was a hard set to the thick-lipped mouth and the dark eyes held intangible hostility in their depths.

'Here's Gus Pank,' Buck said. 'He and

Brunt are sidekicks, and what one doesn't think of in human deviltry the other does. The other two in the gang right now are Jesse Coe and Jake Cowden, and there is no decency in either of them. You've got to go along with the plan, Matt, or there will be mayhem in town tomorrow. You've got to take my word for it.'

'How did you fall in with such a God-awful bunch?' Matt demanded. 'There's no way I can entrust the folks of this town to their mercy. I've got no choice but to get a posse together and stand and fight.'

'Think of the hostages. And Ginny will be among them in the morning.'

'You said one of the gang is out at B Bar waiting for Ginny to leave in the morning.' Matt's thoughts began turning swiftly. 'I could be out there before first light, and get the drop on the killer before he can grab Ginny.'

'You're overlooking Jake Cowden. He's in town watching your movements right now, and he'll plug you the minute you step out of line.'

'You can get to him,' Matt said tensely. 'Get the drop on him and I'll lock him in a cell. That will take care of two of the six, and with only four left I'd have a good chance of whittling them down.'

'But the other four have two hostages already, and Kimber will be waiting with them by the schoolhouse for Jesse Coe to turn up with Ginny.'

'Instead of which I'll have a posse of a dozen men surrounding them.' Matt spoke fiercely. He picked up his pistol from the corner of the desk where Buck had put it. 'You've made a bad mistake, Buck, coming in here thinking you can fool me into submission. There's no way I'd stain my badge and character by going along with you.'

'It's your choice, Brother.' Buck eyes narrowed. 'But I don't think you could live with yourself afterwards if innocent folk get killed in the shoot-out.'

'Will you call out Jake Cowden so I can get the drop on him?' Matt demanded.

Buck shook his head. 'It's more than my life is worth. I wouldn't want to be the one to start a blood bath around here. I couldn't have that on my conscience for the rest of my life. Why don't you take a little time to think about it? You might come up with a different solution when you've given it more thought.'

'I have got some business to take care of,'

Matt said slowly. 'I'll handle that and come back to you. Where can I find you in half an hour?'

'I'll be in the restaurant. Meet me there, and make sure you don't do anything in the meantime to alarm Cowden or he'll put a slug in you.'

'I've got a report of rustling to check on,' Matt said. 'I'll come to the restaurant in thirty minutes and let you know what I've decided.'

Buck nodded and departed. Matt sat gazing at the street door after it had closed behind his brother, his thoughts whirling. Unaccustomed indecision gripped him and he agonized over what he should do. The choice was simple. Either he went along with Eli Kimber's plan and stayed well clear of town during the bank raid or he took a chance with the lives of innocent townsfolk and attempted to capture the gang when they showed up at the bank.

How would Tom Flynn, with his years of experience in law dealing, handle this situation? Matt shook his head, aware that he dared not approach the ailing sheriff for fear of triggering the outlaw watching his movements into action. Whatever he decided to do, he would have to act on his own initiative.

He left the lamp burning in the office when he departed, paused to lock the street door, and had to make an effort not to peer around into the surrounding shadows in case Jake Cowden was watching him. A thought came to him that perhaps Buck was spinning him a yarn about the gang. He might be unobserved! Buck could be playing some deep game of his own. But he could not take that chance and walked briskly through the rain, his chin pulled into the collar of his slicker and his Stetson low over his eyes.

So Hulk Grayson was thinking of buying rustled beeves! Matt considered the fact as he returned to the alley beside the bank which led to the slaughterhouse on the back lots overlooking the river. He paused at the rear of the bank and looked around. Yellow light was emanating from the tall butchery by the river. There were two corrals off to the right, both holding a few steers that were huddling together against the rails, their backs turned to the wind and the rain.

Matt walked through the mud of the back lot and passed the corrals. A steer bellowed forlornly. Matt grimaced. There was a smell of blood emanating from the slaughterhouse which the rain could not dissipate, and the steers in the corrals were uneasy because of it. He mounted a flight of rickety wooden steps to a door and entered an office, which was deserted. An inner door, he knew, led into a storage room, and he crossed to it as he unbuttoned his slicker, and pushed it open.

Hulk Grayson was in the storeroom, a giant of a man in rubber boots and a rubber, blood-spattered apron, who stood at least six feet four inches tall with shoulders like an ox and great hands and massive arms. There was not an ounce of fat on his muscular frame. His large head sat on a thick neck that bulged with muscle. His features were coarse. His bulbous nose was crooked – had been broken more than once in the numerous fights in which he indulged. He was a bully who scared off much of the opposition, and it usually took several men to overpower him when he went on one of his occasional benders and assailed all-comers or attempted to smash up the town.

'Whaddya want?' Hulk's voice was thick and low-pitched, as if it emanated from his boots. He was sweeping down after a day's work. Several sides of beef and various other cuts of meat were suspended from hooks on a rail. He supplied the restaurant and the general store with meat and ran a private trade around the town and surrounding countryside.

'Just to talk right now,' Matt said. 'I've heard that you might be going into business with a couple of rustlers – buying stolen stock cheaply.'

'Who in hell told you that lie?' Hulk slammed down his broom and came across the room with quick steps, moving surprisingly fast for a big man. He clenched his fists into clubs and waved his right fist under Matt's nose.

Matt remained motionless, his bland expression changed, but his right hand was close to the butt of his holstered pistol. He grinned as he met Hulk's furious gaze.

'Don't try to bully me, Hulk,' he warned. 'You're wasting your time. You know that cuts no ice with me. I'm here to warn you friendly-like to be careful. You've got a good business going around here and it would be a pity if you ruined it by taking up with Tarmy and his bunch.'

'Who's been talking to you?' Hulk demanded. 'It's a dirty lie! Someone is out to ruin me.'

'You must have a guilty conscience if you think someone has ratted on you. Well, it doesn't matter where I got my information from. I have it straight from the horse's mouth, and you better change your mind pretty damn quick about your crooked plan or you'll find yourself sitting in a cell, with no future to contemplate.'

'Someone is trying to cause trouble for me.' Hulk crooked his fingers into massive claws and lifted them threateningly toward Matt's face. 'You better tell me who you've been talking to or I'll screw your head off'n your shoulders.'

'I came to warn you off, Hulk,' Matt said quietly. 'If you can't accept that then you're a bigger fool than I took you for.'

'I'm glad you dropped in.' Hulk grinned suddenly, his cavern of a mouth opening to reveal broken, blackened teeth. 'I got a bone to pick with you. I guess you ain't the only one folks talk to. I heard that you and Bella have been getting too friendly. Do you reckon that badge can give you any protection?'

'Stick to the point,' Matt countered. 'I've warned you and you better take notice or you'll be up to your neck in bad trouble.'

'There's bad trouble for you right now,' Hulk roared as his temper flared, and his big hands flashed out to grasp Matt around the throat in a choking grip that threatened to snap Matt's neck like a dry stick...

THREE

Matt drew his pistol swiftly as Hulk's powerful fingers closed around his neck. He jabbed the muzzle against the big man's belly, but Hulk ignored the threat and applied pressure to Matt's throat, cutting off his air. Matt jabbed hard with his gun but to no avail. Hulk was like a maddened bull when he lost his control. Black spots appeared before Matt's eyes and he knew a moment of panic for he was completely helpless in Hulk's grasp. Blackness filled his sight as he swung his pistol up from Hulk's belly and jabbed the muzzle against the man's left shoulder. His senses were receding when he squeezed the trigger and the crash of the shot rang echoingly through the dank slaughterhouse.

Hulk relaxed his grip as the half-inch slug tore into his massive shoulder. He fell back a pace, bellowing like a stricken steer, and then lunged forward again, his hands clenching into fists. His right fist swung ponderously towards Matt's head. Matt ducked and gave ground. Hulk's fist grazed his chin and lights flashed before his eyes but he eased to his left, gasping for breath, and slammed the barrel of his pistol against Hulk's skull. The weapon bounced off as if it had struck a rock. Hulk roared in anger. Blood was seeping out of the bullet wound in his shoulder but he ignored it and pressed forward relentlessly.

Matt was desperate as he ducked a heavy blow. He knew he could not match Hulk man to man. He twisted sideways from another blow and jammed the muzzle of his gun against Hulk's left shoulder-blade as the big man swung away under the surging weight of his own punches. Matt squeezed the trigger a second time. The shot blasted trough the enclosed space, hurling more echoes around the slaughterhouse. The bullet tore through flesh and bone and Hulk staggered, fell to his knees, and then pitched forward on to his face and lay still.

It was all Matt could do to remain upright. He staggered back several paces, covering the big, still figure and, when he realized that Hulk was not foxing, he went forward to examine the slaughterman. Hulk was unconscious. Blood was dribbling out of the hole in his left shoulderblade. Matt saw that the wound was lower down the shoulder than he had anticipated and hoped he had not killed the big man.

He holstered his gun and left quickly, intent on fetching Doc Crickmore, but went no further than the big saloon and peered in over the batwings. Jack Ryder, the bartender, looked up and came along the bar with an expression of anxiety on his smooth face.

'I thought I heard a couple of shots, Matt,' he called. 'Is anything wrong?'

'Get word to Doc Crickmore to go to the slaughterhouse,' Matt rapped. 'Tell him it's urgent. Hulk is down with a couple of slugs in him.'

Matt turned and hurried away with a string of excited questions ringing in his ears. He went back to the slaughterhouse and found Hulk as he had left him – unconscious and breathing heavily.

Boots sounded on the steps leading up to the office and Matt opened the storeroom door to see Tom Flynn lurching into the office, a gun in his hand. The sheriff was unsteady on his feet, his face pale.

'I heard shots,' Flynn said. 'What's going on, Matt?'

'It's nothing I can't handle,' Matt replied.

'By the look of you I'd say you should be in bed.'

He explained the incident and the sheriff went into the storage room, looked at Hulk and then returned to the office.

'I've always known Hulk would come down to this,' Flynn observed. 'A bully like him with such a raging temper, it's a wonder it hasn't happened before. But he looks like he'll live. You reckon he was about to start buying rustled beeves? Who passed that information to you?'

'Bella spoke to me earlier; said she'd overheard Hulk and Jack Tarmy talking about it.'

'Jeez, you better keep that quiet. If Hulk learns his wife turned him in he'll kill her. And you better pick up Tarmy as soon as you can.'

Doc Crickmore came into the office carrying his medical bag.

'Where is he?' he demanded.

'Through here.' Matt led the way into the storeroom and remained in the background while the doctor examined the wounded man.

'You shot him twice!' Crickmore exclaimed.

'It took two slugs to put him down,' Matt

explained. 'He had his hands around my throat and was choking me. It was the only way I could stop him.'

Crickmore got to his feet. 'It'll take more than a couple of slugs to kill Hulk,' he said confidently. 'I'll get some help to move him to my place. Let me take a look at your neck, Matt. I can see bruises from here. It's a wonder Hulk didn't wring your head from your shoulders. You lawmen are going to have to put a curb on Hulk when he's recovered from this or one of these days he will kill someone.'

'We'll take care of it, Doc,' Flynn said wearily.

'You need to start taking care of yourself, Tom,' the doctor responded as he departed. 'I ain't happy about your condition.'

'I'll leave you to it.' Flynn turned away. 'I'll see you in the morning, Matt.'

Hulk groaned and moved and Matt bent over him, but the slaughterman was still unconscious. Matt did not like the thread of thoughts running through his mind as he waited impatiently for the doctor to return with help to move Hulk. Time seemed to stand still as he wrestled mentally with a decision that had to be made before morning. What should he do? How could he even begin to decide when a wrong choice might mean death to some of those people who relied on him for security?

Crickmore returned with four men and the unconscious Hulk was lifted and taken away. Matt went back to the street and stood in the shadows to look around. Could his brother Buck be trusted? Was there an outlaw in town watching his movements? He went to the restaurant and peered in through the big front window to see Buck seated at a corner table chatting and smiling with Rosie, one of the waitresses.

Buck stiffened when Matt walked into the diner. He said something to Rosie, who turned immediately and went back to the kitchen. Matt crossed to Buck's table and stood opposite his brother, looking down at him and wondering what was passing through his devious mind.

'I heard two shots,' Buck said. 'What happened?'

'You know Hulk Grayson.' Matt shrugged. 'I tried to give him a friendly warning and he blew his top. I had to shoot him twice to stop him choking me to death.'

'Is he dead?'

'No! He's stronger than two steers and a buffalo. But this is only the beginning. He'll come for me when he's on his feet again and I reckon I'll have to kill him next time.'

'It's a wonder someone hasn't killed him before this. Have you reached a decision yet?'

'Yes!' Matt suppressed a sigh. 'I'm not gonna toe any line an outlaw draws for me. I'll fight, and I'll be ready when the gang shows up, hostages or no hostages.'

'A lot of innocent folk might get killed in the shooting,' Buck warned.

Matt shook his head. 'That's the way it goes. Now you'd better get out of town and stay out. I don't wanta set eyes on you again, Buck. Start making tracks, and if you've got any sense at all you won't go back to Kimber and his bunch. Head for the nearest border and lose yourself in other parts.'

'You sure sound like you have made up your mind.' Buck got to his feet, his expression bleak. 'I hope you know what you're letting yourself in for.'

'Just get to hell out before I do my civic duty and throw you in a cell.' Matt spoke wearily, and remained motionless with narrowed gaze while Buck considered.

'Watch your back, Brother,' Buck said. 'Cowden is somewhere around, and he'll plug you the minute he suspects you're going against the stream. I don't think you've taken into account all the possibilities in this situation. Do yourself a favour and think about this some more. You've still got time to get it right.'

'To do what you want,' Matt corrected. 'No. I'd be a fool to trust you. Go on and beat it. My duty is plain and nothing will prevent me doing it. You've got five minutes to get out of town. If I see you after the deadline you'll go to jail.'

Buck shook his head and departed swiftly. Matt heaved a sigh, but he felt good about the development. He had to do his job no matter what it cost. If he survived the shoot-out he would be able to live with himself, and that was all that mattered.

He sat down at the table and signalled to Rosie, who was peering at him from around the half-open kitchen door. Tall and blonde, aged twenty-five, she was attractive and had always looked upon Matt with great favour. She came to him, smiling a welcome.

'Hi, Rosie,' he greeted. 'What was my brother talking about? You should take a pinch of salt with anything he says.'

'So he is your brother! He said he was, but I didn't believe him. Come to think of it he does look a lot like you, but he doesn't live around here, he says.'

'No, and he's leaving town right now. I doubt if you'll see him again. Give me a plateful of whatever you've got on hand and make it quick. I've got a lot to do before morning and I haven't eaten since breakfast.'

Rosie hurried hack into the kitchen to return shortly with a large plate loaded with hot food. Matt set to work on the meal and ate it with great relish, finishing off with two cups of coffee. He sat back in his seat to relax for a few moments and his attention was attracted by the street door being opened. A big stranger entered the diner and sat down at a table near the door. Matt ran an eye over him and a thrill of anticipation trickled through his breast. The newcomer looked familiar. Then it came to him. He was looking at Jake Cowden; the outlaw Buck had said was watching him here in town.

Cowden ordered a coffee and sat stirring it casually, but Matt could see the bad man was on edge, his right hand held close to the butt of his holstered gun. Matt wondered if Cowden was of a mind to start shooting, but figured he would have waited outside in ambush rather than risk a confrontation. Perhaps he thought he would not be recognized.

Matt got to his feet and threaded his way

between the small tables, aware that Cowden watched him closely without appearing to do so. The outlaw's right hand dropped below the table top. Matt walked on by but turned swiftly, drawing his pistol as he did so. Cowden started to pull his gun but Matt easily beat him to the draw and pressed the muzzle of his pistol against the nape of Cowden's neck.

'Sit still!' Matt warned. 'You're Jake Cowden, one of Kimber's gang.' He reached down with his left hand and relieved the outlaw of his pistol. 'OK, now get up and head for the jail. I guess you know where it is. Don't try anything, or you'll wind up dead.'

Matt backed off as Cowden got to his fret. Cowden raised his hands and turned to the door, his face frozen in shock. Matt followed, staying just out of reach as Cowden departed, and paused to close the door of the restaurant. He did not relax his vigilance and Cowden did not attempt to resist. They started along the street towards the law office, and Matt was congratulating himself over this latest development when two guns began shooting from the shadows across the street.

Cowden uttered a cry and fell heavily. He

covered Matt inadvertently from the initial shots and Matt dropped to the sidewalk in an instinctive reaction and rolled quickly as shooting hammered and echoed. The speeding slugs tore strips of wood from the sidewalk and thudded into the front of the diner. Orange gun flashes split the shadows across the street. Matt did not stop moving until he had rolled out of the line of fire. He finished up in an alley mouth, and by the time he was ready to trade lead the shooting had ceased.

He lay motionless, regaining his breath and listening to the fading echoes of the shots, shocked by the attack. He heard the sound of feet running away along an alley across the street, and by the time he arose and took a fresh grip on his pistol the noise had faded and silence returned.

Jake Cowden was lying on his face on the sidewalk. Matt gazed at the outlaw for what seemed an interminable time before going forward to check him. He found Cowden dead with a splotch of blood on his face, his inert body dimly illuminated by a straying ray of light from the nearby window of the diner. The outlaw had been hit in the throat and upper body by at least three of the first shots – had inadvertently intercepted those bullets intended for Matt himself

Boots were pounding on the sidewalk and excited voices came to Matt's ears as townsfolk ventured out to investigate the disturbance. Matt drew a deep breath, fought down his shock and came back to full awareness. He stepped back into denser shadows, his finger trembling on the trigger of his pistol.

'What was all the shooting about?' Tom Piercey, the undertaker, came to Matt's side. 'Who's that?' he demanded, gazing down at the inert body.

'He's a customer for you, Tom – an outlaw named Jake Cowden, one of Eli Kimber's gang. I'd just arrested him in the diner and we walked out to the sidewalk into a hail of slugs. I reckon Cowden saved my life, being between me and the ambushers.'

'Did you get a look at the gunnies?' Piercey demanded.

Matt shook his head. 'No. It was too dark. Take care of Cowden, huh?'

'Do you reckon it was more of Kimber's gang shooting at you?' Piercey looked around. 'I'll fetch Bill Spanton. He'll help me remove the body.'

Matt ignored questions from others who came crowding around. He crossed the street and stood in the mouth of the alley from which the shots were fired, wondering at the identity of his attackers. He was inclined to think it had been the handiwork of outlaws for he could not accept that anyone in town would have shot at him. Then he thought of Hulk Grayson planning to buy rustled beeves from Jack Tarmy, and his mind slipped into another angle. Tarmy operated a shoestring cattle ranch north of town with a couple of no-goods, Zeb Grove and Rube Motter.

He knew he would have to pursue that line of enquiry, but pressure was building in the back of his mind. He had to get to B Bar in the morning before Ginny left the ranch for the school on the edge of town, and he would need time to try and locate the outlaw Jesse Coe, who was supposed to be watching for Ginny's departure from the ranch. He wished for daylight so he could check the prints in the alley for sign of the ambushers, but was aware that he would have to be out of town by then.

Footsteps sounded on the sidewalk and he faded into the shadows as a figure appeared. A woman's voice called out urgently.

'Who's there? Is that you, Matt? Don't leave. I need to talk to you.'

Matt waited, having recognized Bella

59

Grayson's voice. She came on and paused before him. A strong smell of cheap perfume caught at his nostrils as she grasped his left arm.

'You didn't have to shoot Hulk, did you?' Bella demanded. 'I asked you to talk to him, warn him that the law knew what he planned so he would pull in his horns and behave himself, but you shot him, and not just once. Doc Crickmore is digging two bullets out of Hulk's shoulder.'

'I was forced to, Bella,' Matt protested. 'The minute I mentioned rustling he attacked me and I had to shoot him to save my life. He got me by the throat and was choking me. The damn fool wouldn't listen to reason.'

'I shouldn't have told you about Hulk's plans,' Bella continued in a bleak tone. 'Now what will happen to Hulk's business? He won't be able to work for weeks and there is no one else can do his job. And if he learns I told you about him he'll surely kill me.'

'Bella, I'm in a hurry right now.' Matt spoke firmly. 'I'll come and talk to you some time tomorrow and we'll see what we can work out.'

'What are you gonna do about Jack Tarmy?'

'What about him?'

'He's the one rustling cows, and when he hears what you've done to Hulk he'll be paying you a visit; him and his two cronies. You better watch your back. You've got yourself into a lot of trouble now, Matt, and all you needed to do was have a quiet word in Hulk's ear!'

'Maybe your warning comes too late, Bella.' Matt grimaced as he glanced around. 'Two guns opened up at me as I left the diner a few minutes ago. Do you know if Tarmy is in town?'

'I was talking to him about the time you shot poor Hulk,' Bella replied. 'He was waiting at my place for Hulk to show up for his meal, and took off fast when Doc Crickmore came to tell me Hulk had been shot.'

'Did Tarmy learn that I shot Hulk?'

'Sure. Doc Crickmore was full of it when he showed up. Nobody but you would go up against Hulk, and the doc was pleased you had put Hulk down. So you better watch your back. I wouldn't want to see you killed because I told you about Hulk.'

'Thanks for the warning. I'll talk to you again later.' Matt began to move away, wanting to look for Tarmy before the man could leave town, but Bella grasped his arm.

'Don't leave me out here alone,' she pleaded. 'I'm scared of the dark. See me home, Matt. I risked everything coming out to warn you. If Tarmy knew I was talking to you there's no telling what he'd do to me. He's poisonous like a rattlesnake.'

Matt turned instantly and Bella tucked her left arm through his right arm as they headed for her home. Matt withdrew his arm and stepped around her, leaving his gun hand free, and Bella hung on to his left arm as if she were afraid he would suddenly run off into the shadows.

'There's big trouble coming around here,' Bella remarked.

'What do you mean? This town has never been quieter, apart from Hulk.'

'Tarmy said he was out by the nester place east of B Bar today, where Frank Wenn runs a few cows, and he saw strangers out there. There were nearly a dozen saddle horses in Wenn's corral, and a couple of men were beating Wenn with their fists while another was holding a knife to Mrs Wenn's throat.'

Matt halted in mid-stride at Bella's words, shocked into immobility.

'Tarmy told you that?' he demanded. 'And he didn't think to come and report it to the law?'

'You know what Tarmy thinks of the law. He wouldn't cross the street to pass the time of day with anyone wearing a tin star.'

Matt drew a deep breath. So that was where Kimber and his gang were right now – out at Wenn's place! Buck said Kimber had taken Wenn and his wife hostage, and the gang must he hiding out there until it was time for them to ride into town to rob the bank.

'Come on, Bella.' Matt hurried the woman along the sidewalk. 'Let's get you home. I've got a lot to do and not much time in which to do it.'

Bella protested at the fast pace for she had to run to keep up with Matt's long strides. When they reached Hulk's home Matt saw the place was in darkness. He moved behind Bella as she produced a key, and muttered impatiently when she fumbled unnecessarily with the lock. He took the key from her and inserted it into the lock. The door swung open and he reached for a match to light the way into the lobby.

'You go in first, Matt,' Bella said nervously. 'I'm afraid of the dark.'

She stepped aside as she spoke and put a hand on Matt's shoulder to propel him forward across the threshold. Matt moved in until he heard the click of a pistol being cocked inside the house. He threw himself flat, reaching for his gun, and the next instant the night was split by rapid gunfire...

FOUR

A bullet nicked the top of Matt's shoulder as he went down and red-hot pain streaked through his flesh. Several more slugs passed through the space he had occupied in the upright position. Two guns were shooting at him from inside the house and he lifted his pistol to return fire. He aimed just above a gun flash to his right and squeezed the trigger, closing his eyes for a split second to avoid the dazzling muzzle flame spurting from the weapon. He rolled to his right and came up into the aim again as a slug tore through the brim of his Stetson just above his right ear.

The thunder of the shots in the close atmosphere of the house was deafening. Matt cocked his gun. He could see nothing in the stretch of darkness. There was no more shooting and he waited tensely, gun ready. As the echoes faded he picked up the sound of someone blundering through the darkness to the back of the house. Then he heard Bella just outside the front door, screeching to be told what was going on.

Matt eased backwards out of the doorway. He stood up and placed his back against the wall beside the open door. His ears were ringing in protest at the shooting and he swallowed a couple of times to relieve them.

'You set me up, Bella,' he accused. 'You pushed me into the house knowing Tarmy was waiting for me.'

'I did not!' Bella replied indignantly. 'I didn't know he was still here. But I told you he would try to get you for shooting Hulk.'

'All right; shut up now.' Matt leaned towards the open doorway. 'Tarmy,' he called, 'come out with your hands up or I'll come in after you, and if I have to do that I'll drag you out feet first.'

He waited for a reply but there was no response and total silence followed his words. He waited a few moments before repeating his ultimatum, but there was no reply and he steeled himself to re-enter the house. He cocked his gun and drew a deep breath.

'You've killed Tarmy!' Bella accused.

Matt ignored her and thrust himself through the doorway into the house, moving fast, his muscles tensed for shooting. He lunged to his left out of the doorway, barged into a corner and dropped to one knee, his pistol cocked and ready. There was no response from inside and he drew a deep breath, reached into a pocket for a match and flicked it into flame with his left thumbnail. He peered around quickly, expecting shots, but there was no response and a sigh escaped him when he saw Rube Motter stretched out on his back with his toes turned up and his pistol lying discarded by his side. There was no sign of Jack Tarmy. The rustler had departed, and Matt was aware that he had to go for the rustler because he would have no peace until Tarmy was settled.

Bella peered in through the doorway and screamed when she saw the inert body. Matt got to his feet and touched his match to the wick of a lamp standing on a nearby table. He holstered his gun and turned to survey the dead man, a silent protest forming in his mind as he tried to grasp what was happening. Buffalo Crossing had been a quiet town until his brother Buck returned, and he knew that what was unfolding now would be as nothing when Kimber and his gang rode in.

Bella moved into the doorway, whimpering at the sight of Rube Motter sprawled in her house.

'You've killed him!' she accused. 'Don't stand there looking at him. Get him out of my house. He's bleeding all over my clean floor.'

'Piercey will move him,' Matt replied curtly. 'If he's heard the shooting he'll be here in a couple of minutes. I think you set me up, Bella!'

He left the house and Bella uttered a squawk and came running after him, clawing at his arm. Matt thrust her away. He saw figures approaching and dropped a hand to his holster, but relaxed when Tom Piercey called out.

'What's going on, Matt? Who's dead now?'

'Motter is lying in Bella's house,' Matt replied. 'Get him out of there, Tom.'

Piercey paused in shock and gazed at Matt as he went on along the street. Matt could hear Bella complaining to the undertaker and closed his ears to the sound of her voice. He was cold with shock. His small world had been turned upside down, and the immediate future looked bleak. He had decided on his action, but was reluctant to carry it through although he knew he had no choice in the matter. His duty had always come first with him and he had to start preparing for the fight which was drawing inevitably nearer with each passing minute.

'Is that you, Matt?' Doc Crickmore called from his doorway as Matt walked by. 'Is there anything I can do? I heard more shooting.'

'It's Tom Piercey's business,' Matt replied. 'Tarmy and Motter were waiting in Hulk's house for me to show up and I killed Motter. Tarmy got away. Bella got me to walk her home. I think she set me up because I shot Hulk. But I've got worse trouble ahead, Doc. I heard that Eli Kimber and his gang are planning to show up here tomorrow and rob the bank. They're out at Frank Wenn's place right now, holding Wenn and his wife hostage.'

Matt went on to explain what he had learned, and felt a certain amount of relief in talking about the problem. Crickmore listened until Matt fell silent, and then cleared his throat.

'What steps are you taking to combat this trouble?' he asked. 'And where is Zeb Grove? If Tarmy and Motter took you on then Grove won't be far away.'

'I haven't seen any sign of Grove. He'll have to wait until later unless he gives me trouble. I thought about riding out to B Bar to warn Ginny to stay away from school tomorrow.' Matt felt doubts fill his mind even as he spoke. 'When the kids find she hasn't showed up they'll go on home again. But Kimber is holding Frank Wenn and his wife hostage, and if I take a posse out to their place they'll likely get killed in the shoot-out.'

'I don't see that you have any choice but to go along with that,' Crickmore said in a matter-of-fact tone. 'If the gang get inside of town limits a lot more folk will die. That bunch raided Broken Horn four months ago and seven people were killed in cold blood before it was over. We don't want that to happen here, Matt. Have you spoken to the sheriff?'

'No. I didn't want to bother Tom, the way he's feeling right now.'

'You'll have to talk to him. If he doesn't know about the raid and hears shots in the morning he'll come out of his house with a gun in his hand and likely get himself killed. Go and tell him about this right now. Don't try to handle it alone. Tom is the top lawman around here and he has a right to know what's going on.'

'You're right.' Matt drew a deep breath to control the thrill of excitement running through him. 'I'll take care of that right away. Thanks for your advice, Doc.'

'I'll go and have a word with Joe Tilney. Being the mayor he has a right to know what is going on. He'll probably call out the regular posse and warn them to be ready to ride with you.'

Matt turned and headed for Flynn's house, eager to get things moving now the decision to act had been taken. There was a light in the sheriff's window, and when he knocked at the door it was opened immediately by Sarah Flynn, the sheriff's wife. She was a tall, thin woman in her early fifties and looked at Matt with worry showing in her careworn expression. Her eyes were watchful and cold as she studied Matt's intent features, seeming afraid of what he had to say.

'How's Tom?' Matt enquired.

'He's not very well, I'm afraid. What's happened, Matt? I heard shooting. You're not going to drag Tom out, are you? He was sleeping peacefully when I looked in on him. He's not at all well and shouldn't be disturbed.'

'I need to talk to him, Sarah. Something has come up that I have to discuss with him.'

Sarah suppressed a sigh and moved back out of the doorway. Matt stepped into the house and followed her up the stairs to the neat little front bedroom. He waited while she touched the shoulder of the still sleeping sheriff. Flynn stirred and opened his eyes.

'Matt is here to talk to you, Tom,' Sarah said.

'Sorry to bother you, Sheriff,' Matt said, as Sarah left the room. 'There's trouble coming up that I think you should know about.' He launched into an account of what had occurred around town after the sheriff had gone off duty earlier, and Flynn closed his eyes as he listened. 'It's a big problem,' Matt ended. 'How do you reckon I should handle it?'

'I'd better get up and take over.' Flynn threw back the bed cover.

'No, you stay where you are,' Matt protested. 'I can handle it. Just tell me what you think is the best way of dealing with it. You're not well enough to step in.'

Flynn got out of bed, staggered, and sat down on the side of the bed. He lowered his head into his hands and stifled a groan.

'I guess you're right,' he said. 'I'd only be a liability to you. Get your posse together and warn them to stand by. Don't let

72

Kimber grab any more hostages.'

'I figured that,' Matt nodded. 'Would it be better to tackle the gang out at Wenn's place, or wait for them to ride into town?'

'Take twenty men out to Wenn's place and surround it. If Kimber and his bunch are there you'll contain them but once they get into town you won't have a chance of taking them without bloodshed.' Flynn spoke decisively. 'Run off their horses if they are at Wenn's place and then you'll have them cold. Don't give them any chances. Kimber's gang are all hardened killers. If they resist you then shoot the hell out of them.'

Matt nodded, fired up by the sheriff's words. He turned to leave, impatient now to get organized.

'Whatever happens, don't let that bunch get into town and grab more hostages,' Flynn said as a parting shot. 'I'll be back on duty in the morning, and I'll have some men staked out around the bank and the street in case Kimber does get by you. We'll be ready for them, Matt.'

Leaving the sheriff's house, Matt discovered that the rain had eased and he straightened his shoulders as he prepared to face the job in hand. He would need all his wits about him. He saw figures along the

73

street converging on the saloon, and when he reached the batwings he discovered the dozen men who usually formed the nucleus of the regular posse gathering inside. Questions were flung at him as soon as he entered the saloon. He saw Doc Crickmore at the bar, talking earnestly with Charles Tarrant, the banker, who was looking badly worried.

'I want at least twenty men to ride with me,' Matt said when the men fell silent to hear his orders. 'Three of you go to the store. Tell Will Carmody we'll need supplies for at least two or three days, and every man better take fifty rounds of ammunition.'

'I heard it is Kimber and his gang,' someone said. 'They're bad medicine, Matt. Can we handle them?'

'Sure we can, if we do it right,' Matt countered. 'Come on, let's get moving. We've got a ten-mile ride and I want to be in position well before dawn.'

'What was all the shooting about earlier?' demanded Gus Redwood, who owned the gun shop. His angular face was grim with suspicion, his dark eyes shining like black pebbles from a creek bottom. 'Was it Kimber's bunch?'

'No. It was not connected with Kimber.'

74

Matt looked around at the intent faces of the men who would have to trade lead with the Kimber gang. Most of them had ridden with a posse on more than one occasion and were accustomed to the duties of posse-men.

'And you're taking out a posse of twenty men each carrying fifty cartridges,' Redwood continued. 'Heck, Matt, I don't know if I've got that many shells in stock.'

'We'll take what you've got,' Matt said.

'I was at the stable earlier,' said Dave Pollard, who owned the diner. His fleshy face was wearing a frown. 'Ben Turner wasn't around, and when I looked in his office I saw bloodstains on his desk. What's going on, Matt? Has something happened to Turner?'

'I've kept quiet about what's been happening around here, Matt,' Doc Crickmore called, 'but you better tell everyone now.'

Matt was conscious of the ensuing silence. He had everyone's attention and all eyes were upon him. He explained the bare facts of Ben Turner's murder and his run-in with Hulk Grayson, Tarmy and Motter. The silence continued, and some of the men began to mutter and shuffle their feet; most of them seeming badly shocked by the news.

'Heck, I don't feel like riding out with the posse and leaving my family here un-protected,' Gus Redwood protested. 'Kimber's bunch could likely be outside town right now, watching and waiting for a posse to ride out, and they'd have the place at their mercy with us gone. Our first duty is to our families, Matt. Why do we have to ride out to tackle the outlaws? We could catch them cold in the street when they ride in tomorrow.'

'I've talked to the sheriff and he agrees we should hit the gang outside of town when they least expect it,' Matt said patiently. 'I know for a fact that Ben Turner was mur-dered this afternoon by one of Kimber's gang; a man named Crazy Joe Stott.'

'Where did you get your information from?' Redwood demanded.

'I can't tell you that at the moment.' Matt shook his head. 'Now let's get organized. I want to be riding out of town in two hours.'

Matt went to Doc Crickmore's side. Charles Tarrant, the banker, looking extremely tense, grasped Matt's arm tightly. His lined face was pale and his blue eyes showed uncertainty.

'Are you sure the gang is coming in to rob the bank tomorrow, Matt?'

'That's the information I've got.' Matt nodded. 'But don't worry about it. The sheriff will be on duty in the morning and he'll have enough men to cover the bank and the street. I expect to nail the gang out of town, but if they do get past my posse they'll be stopped cold in their tracks the minute they hit town. There's no way half-a-dozen outlaws can walk in here and raid the bank if the town is ready and waiting for them.'

'I can't take that chance.' Tarrant's lips hardly moved when he spoke. 'I'd better take the money out of the bank during the night, after the posse has left town, then whatever happens here tomorrow, Kimber won't get his hands on it.'

'If you can get hold of three or four men you can trust to guard the money then that might be a good idea.' Matt shook his head doubtfully. 'Personally I wouldn't want to take that chance, but you run the bank so you should know what to do. I think it would be better to have guards inside the bank in case Kimber gets through the posse.'

Tarrant shook his head indecisively. He was clearly a very worried man.

Doc Crickmore signalled to the bartender and ordered a drink.

'I'll join you in the bank tomorrow morning,' Crickmore said to Tarrant. 'You've got your bank staff. Make sure they are armed, and we'll give a good account of ourselves should Kimber show up. The people weren't ready in Broken Horn when the gang went there, but we shall have a very different story to tell.'

Matt declined a drink and left the saloon, his mind seething with thoughts of what he had to do. Tackling the Kimber gang would be no push-over, he was aware, and wished the sheriff was well enough to lead the posse. But Flynn would cover the town and the posse would outnumber the gang so with surprise on their side they should succeed in stopping the outlaws.

He went to the law office and sat down at the desk to study the posters of the gang, impressing their features upon his mind, and then began to consider the next stage of the counter measures he would employ. If the posse could get into position around Wenn's place and trap Kimber and his gang inside then the rest should be relatively easy, but he dared not think of the two hostages or the consequences if the posse should fail to contain the outlaws.

The street door creaked open and Matt

looked up to see Zeb Grove stepping over the threshold with a drawn pistol in his hand. Grove cocked his gun and Matt sat back in his seat, his eyes cold and watchful. Grove came forward a couple of paces, his gun unwavering. He was a small man with short arms and legs and an immensely powerful body. His fleshy face wore an expression of intense determination.

'Hold it right there, Grove,' Matt said. 'I don't know how deeply you were involved with Tarmy and Grayson, but if you go ahead with what I think you've got in mind then you'll end up with a rope around your neck. You'd better think about that before you make another move.'

'You killed Motter!' Grove's thin lips opened and closed like a trap.

'Tarmy and Motter set an ambush for me; opened fire without warning, and got what they asked for. Hulk was the same. I tried to give him a friendly warning but he attacked me. I knew about Tarmy's plan to supply stolen beeves to Grayson and, as you are one of Tarmy's business partners, I suspect you were aware of the deal Tarmy cooked up with him. I'll know more about that when I catch Tarmy. I doubt the law could prove anything against you right now. But shoot me and you'll be hunted down and charged with murder. As it stands you've got a chance to turn around, get out of here, and make a clean start elsewhere.'

'I've got nowhere else to go.' Grove shook his head obstinately. He was the type of man who, having made up his mind to a certain course of action, would follow it to hell and gone. 'I don't have a choice, Cameron. There's too much evidence lying around. I tried to keep Tarmy in line but he never cared about the consequences. Now he's put himself in bad trouble and I've got to pick up the pieces of what's left of the business. That ain't gonna work so my first chore is to put you out of circulation.'

Matt lifted a hand, palm outwards, and his voice was harsh and tense when he spoke.

'Don't be a fool, Grove. Get to hell out of here. I've got too much on my plate right now to worry about you. Go on and beat it while you've got the chance.'

'No dice!' Grove shook his head stubbornly. 'I'll handle what I've got to do. Put your hands flat on the desk and don't make a move or you'll get it right here and now. I've got it all worked out. We're leaving town. I'm gonna shoot you out at Tarmy's place and bury you under a cut-bank. No one will ever find you. Now do like I tell you. Get your hands spread out on the desk.'

Matt looked into the black muzzle of Grove's unwavering gun and heaved a sigh as he placed his hands on the desk. Grove came around to his side, jerked Matt's pistol from its holster and backed off out of reach.

'Now get a pair of handcuffs and put them on your wrists with your hands behind your back.' Grove waggled his pistol in Matt's face. 'Don't even think of trying something because I'll kill you right here if I have to. Get moving.'

Matt pulled open a drawer in the desk and picked out a set of handcuffs. Under Grove's intent gaze he closed a cuff around his left wrist and put his hands behind his back to snap the other cuff around his right wrist. Grove did not notice there was a key in the lock of the right cuff and Matt removed it and concealed it in his right hand as he snapped the cuff around his wrist with his hands behind his back.

'Turn around and let me see the cuffs on,' Grove ordered and Matt obeyed, his fingers clenched around the key to the handcuffs. 'That's good,' Grove commented, ensuring that the cuffs were fully locked. 'Now let's get outa here. I've got a couple of horses outside. You and me are gonna take a ride and I'll be the only one coming back. It'll be a one-way trip for you.'

When Matt was slow getting to his feet Grove grasped his right elbow, pulled him upright and pushed him towards the door

'Don't make the mistake of yelling for help out on the street,' Grove said. 'I'll cut you down before anyone can hear you.'

Matt walked to the door and opened it, standing outlined for a moment against the lamp light at his back. Grove pushed his gun muzzle against Matt's spine and Matt stepped out to the sidewalk. Two horses were tethered to a nearby hitch rail and Grove chivvied Matt to them.

'You ride the bay.' Grove stuck the muzzle of his pistol under Matt's nose. 'I'll help you into the saddle, but don't try anything or you'll die right here.'

Matt glanced around the street. He saw figures moving around – possemen preparing to ride out to Wenn's place, but he was alone and helpless. Grove thrust him into the saddle and held the bay's reins as he mounted his own horse. He started across the street to an alley opposite the jail and they were soon swallowed up in the darkness. When they reached the back lots

Grove pushed the horses into a canter and they left town quickly.

Desperation filled Matt as they hit the open range for he had vital work to do and the last thing he needed was to be sidetracked by a vengeful killer.

FIVE

Grove remained silent as he led Matt's horse through the night. The rain had ceased but a chill wind was blowing from the north despite the fact that spring was in the air. Matt, his hands manacled behind his back, manipulated the handcuffs key carefully, afraid he might drop it as he worked at getting it into the lock of the left-hand cuff. Grove was just a black figure a few feet ahead and did not turn to check his prisoner, satisfied that the cuffs rendered him helpless. The jolting saddle did not help Matt as they rode at a canter through the night, but slowly he managed to unlock the cuff and remove it from his wrist.

He used the key to unlock the cuff around his right wrist and a thrill of anticipation ran through him as he prepared to tackle Grove. He hung the cuffs over his saddle horn and put the key into his breast pocket. He kicked his feet out of his stirrups and lunged forward out of his saddle, hurling himself at Grove. Matt's outstretched left hand encircled Groves neck while his right hand went to the man's waist, his fingers seeking the butt of Grove's holstered pistol.

Grove uttered a shocked yell as he was grabbed. Matt's momentum took them both to the right and Grove kicked his feet free of his stirrups as he was carried out of the saddle. Matt swung his legs forward and landed on his feet with Grove's pistol in his hand. Grove went head-first to the ground, but bounced to his feet like a rubber ball, his hands doubling into fists and lifting to strike.

Matt struck at Grove's head with the barrel of the pistol but Grove's Steson deflected the blow. Grove threw a wild right-hand punch that caught Matt flush on the left temple and lights flashed in Matt's brain. Thrusting Grove's pistol into his own holster, Matt grappled with Grove, smothering the man's punches. He used his superior weight to good effect, and threw a looping left hand that took Grove full on the chin. Grove gasped and stepped back, but Matt was too desperate to give him any kind of a chance.

He drew the pistol again and slammed the barrel against the side of Grove's head, and then struck again. Grove took the second blow on the temple and uttered a groan as he fell unconscious to the wet ground. Matt straightened, breathing heavily. The two horses had stopped with trailing reins and were standing patiently a few feet away. Matt bent over Grove, the pistol ready in his hand, but the man was unconscious and Matt straightened and fetched the hand-cuffs from his saddle horn.

When Grove recovered his senses he was astride his horse with his hands cuffed behind his back and Matt was riding back to Buffalo Crossing.

'You're a damned fool, Grove,' Matt observed. 'You had a chance to pull out of this but you went the wrong way. Now you're heading for jail, and I'll throw the book at you. You'll be behind bars a long time, and Tarmy will join you when I can get around to arresting him.'

Grove made no reply and Matt took no chances on the short ride back to town. When they entered the street there was a bunch of saddle horses standing in front of the law office, which was filled to over-flowing with impatient possemen.

'Where the hell have you been, Matt?' Gus Redwood demanded. 'We've been ready to ride for the last half-hour. Time is getting away.'

Matt pushed Grove towards the cells and picked up the cell keys.

'What are you jailing Grove for?' someone asked.

'He was fixing to kill me. Has anyone seen Jack Tarmy around town lately? I need to put him behind bars.'

'I saw him about thirty minutes ago,' Redwood said. 'He came into my store for some cartridges – said he was going hunting.'

'Hunting me probably,' Matt said.

He locked Grove in a cell and jangled the keys as he went back into the office. Several of the possemen were looking at the wanted posters of the Kimber gang.

'We've borrowed horses from the livery stable,' Redwood said. 'You'll see that Mrs Turner gets paid, huh, Matt?'

'I'll take care of it,' Matt agreed. 'If everyone is ready then let's hit the trail. We need to be in position well before dawn.'

'I saddled your horse for you,' Redwood said. 'It's waiting outside.'

'Thanks.' Matt took his Winchester from the rifle rack on the back wall of the office and a box of shells from a cupboard nearby. He glanced at the clock. The time was almost midnight. He checked the gun he had taken from Grove and stuck it in his waist-band when he found his own weapon in a corner where Grove had tossed it earlier.

The posse assembled outside in the street. There was very little talking among the men. Most had ridden with a posse before and knew what was expected of them. Matt swung into his saddle and moved out, leading the way, and there was a clatter of hoofs as the possemen strung out behind him. They left town quickly and Matt made a bee-line for Frank Wenn's place.

The wind was chill but there was no rain. Matt rode steadily and the posse remained in a compact group as it continued. Matt's mind was fixed on the coming confront-ation, and he pondered on what he saw as problems to a successful conclusion to the situation. He looked at the situation from every conceivable angle, and was satisfied that he had covered everything.

When they drew near to Wenn's place, a smallholding consisting of a cabin, a barn and a corral beside a meandering stream, Matt called a halt. The posse dismounted and gathered around him for final orders. The night was dark and clouds scudded overhead, chivvied by a stiff breeze. Their range of vision was poor despite the fact that their eyes were accustomed to the gloom. Dawn was still several hours away.

Matt split his posse into three groups, two of which would surround Wenn's cabin while the third party would sneak into the corral and drive off the horses. An ultimatum would be given to the gang when it began to stir at daybreak. If the outlaws resisted they would be assailed with no quarter given.

'We'll keep it simple,' Matt said, 'and then nothing much can go wrong. You can all settle down now and stay quiet in case Kimber has a guard out. I'm going to work my way in close to check out the place, so stay quiet and be ready for anything.'

They were well out of earshot of the cabin and Matt departed quickly to scout the area. He moved in on foot, his Winchester in his hands, and peered around into the dense shadows, unable to make out any details of the cabin by the stream. He soon reached a position from which he could hear the gurgling of the running water and paused to listen intently for unnatural sounds.

The wind moaned in Matt's ears as he surveyed the area. The outline of the cabin was stark. There was no light anywhere to relieve the shadows and the heavy silence seemed to throb against his ears. He circled the cabin to approach the corral. A horse stamped and whinnied, apparently disturbed by his approach, and Matt froze his movements and dropped to the wet grass to check for a guard. His temples throbbed with anticipation as he looked around for movement but the tense moments passed silently and without incident.

When he was satisfied there was no guard around the place he got to his feet and moved in a crouching run to the corral, fetching up against the rails and peering between them. He could see well enough to note only two horses in the enclosure where he was expecting at least a dozen, and he gazed in disbelief, as if unable to accept the evidence of his eyes. Where were the horses belonging to the gang? Had Kimber pulled out?

Disappointment trickled through Matt's mind as he continued around the little spread. There was no movement anywhere and he gazed at the darkened cabin, wondering what he would find inside. He made his way back to where the posse waited.

When he explained the situation there were groans of disappointment from the men, and Matt ignored the questions that came at him.

'Mount up,' he ordered. 'We're riding in to surround the place and check it out. Let's get moving, and make it quick.'

The possemen were only too eager to comply. They mounted and set off for the cabin, their hoofs drumming sullenly on the wet range. Matt rode straight into the yard and reined in while the posse circled the cabin and sat their mounts with levelled weapons in their hands. Matt waited until they were in position and then raised his pistol and fired a shot skywards. He waited for the echoes to fade before calling loudly.

'Hello the cabin! I'm Matt Cameron, the deputy sheriff from Buffalo Crossing. I have a posse of twenty men out here. Light a lamp and come on out with your hands up.'

The silence seemed overwhelming as they awaited a reaction, and when Matt realized there would be no response he heaved a sigh, aware that he had to do this the hard way. He dismounted, trailed his reins, and then drew his pistol and checked it, his movements deft in the shadows.

'Cover me,' he ordered the men nearest to him, and walked across the yard to the door of the cabin.

He was aware of tension building up

behind his breastbone as he stood to one side of the door of the cabin and reached out with his left hand to try it. The door creaked open and he tightened his grip on his levelled pistol. The impenetrable blackness of the interior of the cabin baffled his gaze and he strained his ears for sound.

'Is anyone in there?' he called.

He heard a sound which he could not immediately identify – like a muffled cry of someone trying to talk through a gag, and stepped into the open doorway and moved swiftly to his left to clear the line of fire. The silence was intense. He reached for a match with his left hand and his right index finger was trembling on his trigger when he struck the match. Nothing happened and he heaved a sigh of relief as he looked around in the dim light to locate a lamp.

There was a table to his left and he saw a lamp on it and crossed quickly to light the wick. Yellow glare flooded the cabin and he peered around, his gaze attracted instantly by movement on a bed in the opposite corner of the large room. Two figures were lying on the bed, both hogtied and gagged, and he crossed to them, recognizing the nester Frank Wenn and his wife.

Matt removed Wenn's gag and the man

burst into a torrent of excited speech.

'Take it easy,' Matt cautioned. 'I heard Kimber's gang was here.'

Wenn sat up. He was old, in his fifties, and lean. His angular face was severely bruised and bloodied, his left eye almost completely closed.

'That crooked bunch was here, Matt,' Wenn said. 'They gave me a helluva time because I didn't have any money. They planned on sticking around until tomorrow when they were going into town to hit the bank. They didn't make any secret of their plans. They were going to hold Lizzie and me hostage, and grab Ginny Benton and some of the kids from the school when they showed up there in the morning. I was scared for our lives, I can tell you.'

'So where are the outlaws now?' Matt demanded.

'They pulled out quick when one of their men showed up just after dark. It was your brother Buck, Matt. I got the shock of my life when I recognized him. He'd been in town and came back with the news that one of the gang had been killed on the street. Kimber accused Buck of laying a trap for the gang, and beat him badly, but he denied everything until they searched him and

94

found a cable in his pocket which he must have picked up from the telegraph office in town. It was addressed to him from the Pinkerton Detective Agency in Cheyenne. Buck admitted it then. He said he was working for Alan Pinkerton and had been after Kimber for weeks.'

Matt's brain reeled under the shock of Wenn's words. Buck working for the law! He stifled a groan as he considered. Why had Buck concealed the truth? They could have worked together to nail Kimber and the gang.

'So what happened when Kimber learned that Buck was trying to trap him?' he demanded.

'Kimber called off the bank raid. He figured there would be a bunch of detectives waiting to grab the gang when they showed up in town.'

'And what did they do about Buck?'

'They took him along as a prisoner. Kimber said they would use him for target practice when they got back to the hideout.'

Matt fought against his shock and went to the door of the cabin to call his men in. He ordered two of them to mount guard around the spread while the rest turned their horses into the corral and then bedded down in the barn. Matt considered what he had learned.

'We're staying here till daylight,' Matt told them, 'then we'll pick up the tracks of the gang and go after them. I have been told exactly where their hideout is, and if they are heading in that direction we'll go right along there and take them. There's nothing we can do until morning so settle down and be ready to ride as soon as we can check out the ground.'

Frank Wenn asked for horses to be hitched to his wagon. He was determined to take his wife to town. Mrs Wenn was badly shocked by her experience at the hands of the gang and Wenn himself looked as if he needed medical attention.

'I'll send a couple of men to town with you,' Matt decided. 'And you'd better stay there until we've captured the gang.'

'You'll never take them alive,' Wenn said. 'I never saw a worse bunch of no-goods. Killers, all of them! One really scared me. The others called him Crazy Joe. He looked like he'd kill and skin his own mother if he got half a chance. He stood holding a knife against Lizzie's throat while Kimber worked me over with his fists. I thought our last moments had come, I can tell you. I didn't think we'd be alive by the time they left. I'm surprised they didn't kill us. Kimber said something about coming back after he'd checked for a Pinkerton trap so I want to get out of here before he shows up again.'

Matt arranged for the wagon to be readied, and he was relieved when it pulled out with the Wenns aboard. Two of the possemen went along, one of them driving the wagon, and then Matt settled down to await the coming of dawn. His mind was seething with speculation as he considered the turn of events. He could not get over the fact that his brother Buck was apparently working for Alan Pinkerton.

He wished now he had trusted Buck when he had the chance. He did not doubt that Kimber would kill his brother, and knew he could not afford to take any chances. He needed to get on the trail of the gang immediately. If Kimber had decided to return to his hideout then precious time could be saved by heading in the same direction without delay. Daylight was not due for several hours, and waiting around until dawn did not appeal to Matt. He could be many miles along the trail in the direction of the gang's hideout by dawn if he rode on alone, and time was imperative if he hoped to save his brother's life.

Matt went to the barn and spoke with Gus Redwood, who agreed with Matt's plan without hesitation.

'What have you got to lose?' Redwood demanded. 'You could take a couple of men with you and head for the place you think the gang will be, and in the morning I'll follow your tracks with the rest of the posse. Either way we should come up with the gang.'

Matt nodded, and relief filled him as he saddled his horse. He decided to ride alone, and set out immediately into the night. Buck's description of the place which the gang used as a hideout was in the forefront of his mind and he knew exactly where it was, having hunted and chased criminals through the area on more than one occasion. He had in fact arrested two rustlers in the very same hideout more than a year before.

Dawn found Matt a dozen miles north and quite close to Antelope Creek. He paused for food and coffee as a weak sun came up, and looked around to get his bearings. After eating he pushed on, angling east slightly and, when he came upon the game trail which he needed to follow, he saw fairly fresh tracks of six horses that were ahead of him by a few short hours. He assumed the tracks belonged Kimber's men, and it looked as if the outlaws were going back to their hideout. He wondered how Buck was faring at the hands of the brutal gang.

Matt did not spare his black on the hard ride north. Aware of the murderous tendencies of the outlaws, he was afraid of arriving too late to save his brother, and made good time during the morning. He had no need to track the six horses ahead of him and could tell by the depth of their hoofs in the soil ground that they were not losing any time. He kept an anxious eye on the sun, wanting to reach the hideout before darkness closed in to have a chance of scouting through the area.

He hoped the posse was making good time in following, although they were several hours behind and could not possibly arrive in time to do anything positive about Buck's predicament. Matt was only too aware that it was down to him to rescue his brother.

Daylight was fading when he saw the tracks of a herd of steers angling on to the game trail he was following. He reined in and looked around. The tracks of the steers continued along the game trail and were followed by the prints of the six horses which Matt had assumed belonged to Kimber's gang. He gazed ahead but could see nothing, and it was in his mind that the steers were being herded by rustlers. He clenched his teeth as he imagined unexpected problems arising from the herders.

He reached a spot in broken country where he would have to leave his horse and continue on foot. The hideout was very close and he was afraid of alerting a possible guard to his presence. He left the black knee-hobbled in a side gully, took his rifle, and moved in cautiously, following the tracks left by the steers. Shadows crawled in around him as he moved slowly, ready for any exigency. When he heard the bawling of cattle somewhere ahead he slipped forward from rock to rock, ears and eyes strained. A cold wind moaned through the jumbled rocks.

Darkness finally closed in and he slowed his approach almost to a crawl. He caught the smell of wood-smoke drifting along the gully and got down on all fours when he reached a widening of the narrow pass. He recalled the spot exactly from his previous visit. There was grass ahead in a natural bowl off to the right in the stretch of rocks, and a stream meandered through the area from higher ground to the north. He saw a small fire burning in the entrance to a cave on the left, and heard the sound of horses but could not see them. Then he spotted a guard walking slowly around the area, a rifle clutched in his hands. The man was taking his job seriously, looking about alertly and checking his surroundings meticulously.

Matt lay motionless behind a rock and studied the area. He was aware that the hide-out Buck had mentioned was still ahead by a couple of hundred yards, and wondered what Kimber and his gang were doing. Did the outlaws permit other criminals to use the area? He saw a man cooking at the fire, and the smell of frying bacon reached his nostrils. He was too far away to be able to identify the man and eased forward behind a rock that was much closer to the fire.

Recalling the wanted posters he had seen of the Kimber gang, Matt was unable to identify the cook and assumed the man was one of the herders. It troubled him that none of the outlaws was around. He knew the exact location of the main cave where he expected Kimber to be, and began considering the problems facing him. He needed to get to Buck, put a gun in Buck's hand, and then, together, they would shoot the hell out of the gang. But the cattle herders complicated the situation and Matt fought to control his nagging impatience. He crawled in closer to the fire to watch, keenly aware that while he hesitated his brother could be living out his last moments on earth.

After some minutes the cook took his pots and pans off the fire and turned towards the cave mouth to yell that the meal was ready. Matt narrowed his eyes when three men emerged from the cave, and shock struck him hard when he recognized one of them as Jack Tarmy!

What was Tarmy doing out here with a herd of cattle? Matt shook his head, fully aware of Tarmy's rustling activities. They had traded lead in Bella Grayson's house the night before when Rube Motter was killed. So Tarmy had left town immediately afterwards, and his nefarious undertakings had led him to the very spot where Matt had no wish to see him. But was Tarmy in league with the outlaws?

Matt wished he had time to investigate the riddle, but he was only too aware that Buck's time could be running out and his brother's life was precious to him. He eased back from his cover and began to circle the rustler camp. Tarmy would have to wait. Matt needed to get to grips with Kimber and his murderous bunch before they got around to killing Buck.

Inch by inch, Matt crawled away from the rustler camp. He lay motionless behind a rock while the rustler guard walked silently by without spotting him, and when the man's back was turned Matt edged away to the right. When it was safe to do so he arose and walked steadily up the gully, hoping he was not too late to save Buck. He heard a horse whinny some distance ahead and slowed his pace, certain the outlaws would be on high alert.

Presently he came upon a large fire burning right in the mouth of a big cave in the left-hand wall of the gully. Six horses were standing in dense shadows to the right of the cave with their reins tied to a picket line stretched between two rocks. A man holding a rifle was sitting on a flat rock by the fire.

Matt crouched in the shadows and watched for some moments, his mind busy on the situation. This was the main outlaw hideout and Buck had said there was a back way out of the cave which led into another gully at the rear. If Buck was a prisoner in the cave then where was he exactly? Matt knew he could not pass the guard in the cave entrance and wondered if he could enter through the back way. He came to the conclusion that he had no choice but to try.

He eased back across the gully before getting to his feet, and then the first step he took brought his descending foot down hard on a sharp rock which turned quickly under his weight. He lost his balance and fell heavily sideways while the rock grated harshly as it rolled from under his foot.

Matt dropped into cover but the slight sound alerted the guard instantly. A rough voice called out a challenge which was followed immediately by a shot. Matt ducked as a slug flattened against a rock close by his right shoulder before screaming away into the shadows. The guard had fired blind but the bullet almost hit Matt, and he was badly disconcerted as he ducked away into deeper cover.

SIX

The guard got to his feet and moved forward in the cave mouth until the fire was behind him. Matt watched with narrowed gaze, listening to the fading echoes of the shot. He had drawn his pistol but had no intention of returning fire. A figure emerged from the cave and paused beside the guard. Matt was only a dozen yards away and heard their harsh voices clearly.

'What the hell are you shooting at, Brunt?' the newcomer demanded.

'I heard something out there, Eli, and it wasn't a coyote. Someone is moving around.'

'Have you checked the prisoner? I told you to keep an eye on him. He's full of tricks. Perhaps he's got loose.'

'I'll check him out now, boss.' Wiley Brunt turned to the fire, picked up a short length of wood and stuck one end into the flames. Using the piece of wood as a torch, he held it shoulder high and moved to where the horses were picketed.

Matt caught his breath when he saw a human figure roped to the picket line beyond the sixth horse, and his teeth clicked together when he recognized his brother Buck!

'Was it you making some noise, Buck?' Brunt demanded, thrusting the torch close to Buck's face.

Buck's reply was unintelligible to Matt who saw well enough by his brother's battered and bruised features that he had been beaten severely.

Brunt went back to the cave mouth and tossed the burning brand into the fire before resuming his seat on the flat rock. Eli Kimber turned and faded into the cave. Matt began to crawl in Buck's direction, inching through the scattered rocks in the gully. He skirted the horses and approached Bucks position, unable to see his brother in the shadows. The strewn rocks hurt his knees and elbows but he persevered and paused when he was within whispering distance of the prisoner

'Buck!' Matt whispered the name, his gaze upon Brunt seated in the cave mouth.

'Matt? Is that you?' Buck hissed in reply. 'I figured you'd be out here pretty quick. I heard you coming, and it's a wonder you

106

didn't wake everyone, the noise you were making.'

Matt pulled his knife from its sheath on the back of his pants belt and moved in closer. He caught a pale gleam of reflected firelight on his brother's battered face.

'Let's get you out of here,' he said softly, feeling for the rope binding Buck's hands. 'We'll wait for my posse to show up and then move in on the gang.'

'I don't want to lose them now we have them together.' Buck rubbed circulation back into his wrists when he was free. 'Give me a gun. Matt, and we'll start the shooting right now.'

'I heard you're working for the Pinkerton Agency, Buck. It's a pity you didn't tell me about that when we were talking back in town.'

'I'll give you my whole life story when this is over,' Buck replied, 'but right now let's get this done with.'

'There are four rustlers back along the gully,' Matt warned. 'Does Kimber share this place with them?'

'Anyone outside the law is free to come and go around here. We've got to move fast, Matt. Kimber plans to ride out again after sunup. He's still going for the bank in

Buffalo Crossing, but it will be the day after tomorrow. Once he gets a bee in his bonnet about something he can't get rid of it and he's hooked on the bank in town. When he does go in there he'll make the folks suffer, so he said.'

'There were six in the gang,' Matt mused. 'Jake Cowden was killed in town so are the other five here in the cave?'

'Four of them are – Kimber, Pank, Stott and Brunt. Jesse Coe is out at B Bar, waiting for Ginny to leave for school in the morning. He'll grab her as planned, even though the raid has been put back a day. Kimber plans to be at the schoolhouse in the afternoon the day after tomorrow, and figures to walk into the bank just before closing time.'

Matt uttered an imprecation. 'I thought Coe wouldn't go for Ginny because Kimber called off of his plan,' he said.

'No one went to B Bar to call Coe off. He'll take Ginny as planned and hold her until the raid does go ahead.'

'Then I've got to get the hell out of here and ride hell for leather to B Bar!' Matt grasped Buck's arm and tugged his brother into movement. 'Let's get back to where I left my horse.'

'I'd rather walk in on the gang now,' Buck

108

protested. 'It's a golden chance to catch them altogether. We could get the drop on them and have them hogtied and waiting when your posse shows up.'

'No.' Matt shook his head. 'That's not the way to do it. Either of us might get shot and Kimber would come out on top. I can't afford to take any chances with Ginny being involved. I'll head out fast for B Bar and you can wait by that big rock, which is where I told my posse to meet up with me. When the posse shows up you can guide them in here for a showdown with Kimber and his gang.'

'Kimber won't be here by that time. We've got to do this my way, Matt.'

'You're in no position to make terms. This could have been avoided if you had played it straight with me. Why didn't you warn us of your law activities?'

'I couldn't blow my cover. I was with the gang, acting as one of them, and I made a mistake when I took the opportunity to check the telegraph office in Buffalo Crossing. Kimber didn't trust me an inch, and when I left you and went back to Wenn's place with the news that Cowden had been shot, Kimber searched me and found a wire I had received from Pinkerton's office in Cheyenne.'

'Wenn told me about that,' Matt said. 'Come on, we're getting out of here. Play it my way, Buck, or don't play at all. I want this gang as much as you do, but I'm concerned about innocent folks getting hurt so this is how it's got to be done.'

Matt eased away from the outlaw cave and Buck accompanied him without further protest. It was almost impossible to move silently over the rocky ground but they drew away from the fire in the cave mouth and headed down the gully. A steer bawled angrily from the grassy bowl where the herd was penned. Matt indicated the cave mouth where the rustlers were and they moved on inch by inch until a harsh voice growled at them only feet away to their right.

'Who in hell are you two, and what are you doing prowling around here in the dark? Don't move. I got a gun on you. Blink and you'll draw a slug apiece.'

'Who are you?' Matt countered swiftly. 'Does Kimber know you're using his place?'

'Tarmy saw him earlier and he said there was no problem,' the guard replied. 'But there could have been trouble the way you two almost walked into me.'

'We're checking out the area,' Matt continued. 'I'm glad to see you're on your toes. We'll sing out when we come back.'

'I'll be on the look-out for you,' the guard replied.

Matt moved on with Buck following him closely and the guard accompanied them for a few yards before turning away. Matt heaved a sigh of relief, and when they were clear of the rustlers he turned his head to speak to his brother but his words were drowned out by the blast of a pistol. Five shots tore through the darkness and whined away overhead. Voices yelled through the echoes, and Matt grasped Buck's arm and hunted cover in some rocks. They lay motionless, listening to the dying echoes of the shooting. A voice was yelling angrily. Buck leaned across to Matt and spoke hoarsely.

'That's Kimber shouting. He must have missed me from the picket line.'

'So let's get out of here.' Matt got to his hands and knees. He could hear insistent voices behind them. 'Keep low, Buck,' he warned.

They skittered down the gully on their hands and knees, not caring about the noise they made because two guns began firing at them and bullets whined over their heads or smacked sullenly into surrounding rock.

Matt kept going, aware that shortly the gully bent to the left and they would be safe to lose themselves in the darkness. Buck stayed with him, using the noise Matt made to guide him in the right direction. The gully reverberated with the blaring reports of the guns.

Passing around the bend took them out of the line of direct fire and Matt paused to get his breath. Buck cannoned into him and they fell to the ground.

'Are you OK, Buck?' Matt demanded.

'I'm still in one piece,' his brother replied breathlessly, 'but how long I'll remain like that depends on those galoots back there. I can hear them coming after us. We'd better keep moving, unless you've decided to shoot it out with them.'

'Let's go.' Matt pushed himself erect and made for the end of the gully where it emerged from the slope onto the plain. 'There's a moon up here and we'll be in its light when we get clear of this.'

'I don't suppose you've got a spare horse with you,' Buck said with a chuckle. 'Mine is back there at the cave.'

'We can ride double to that big rock I mentioned and I'll drop you off there. I'm gonna have to push on to B Bar, but I'll never make it before Ginny leaves for school. If Jesse Coe grabs her I'll have to trail him.'

'I'd rather borrow a gun and have a show-down right now,' Buck protested.

'No dice! There are nine hardcases back there and you wouldn't have a chance against them. I don't want to come back and find you dead, Buck. Now let's get out of here before Kimber shows up.'

Their range of vision increased drastically when they left the cover of the gully and were bathed in moonlight. Matt looked around, his pistol ready in his right hand. He handed his Winchester to Buck.

'It's fully loaded,' he advised.

Buck levered a shell into the breech.

'I'm ready for them now,' he replied.

'Stay close to me.' Matt turned and half ran across the rough ground to where he had left his black. Moonlight silvered the rocks and put dense black shadows in the many hollows. When more shooting erupted behind them he dropped flat and squirmed around to face the threat. Buck went to ground beside him.

'We're not gonna get away from them,' Buck observed. 'Kimber won't let up until he's got hold of me again. But this place is as good as any for a fight so let them come close and we'll feed them some lead.'

'I've got a long way to go before the sun shows,' Matt said urgently. 'I need to pick up Coe's tracks at B Bar and take Ginny from him.'

'Head for your horse then and I'll hold them here. Just give me some spare shells for the rifle.'

'There's a box of .44-.40 in my saddle-hag, and a spare pistol. Come on.'

They waited until the shooting dwindled away and then moved out fast, but their movements attracted more shots and Matt ducked when a near miss whined by his right ear. He kept moving and Buck stayed with him. The black showed up where it had been left and Matt quickly prepared the animal for travel. When he was ready to ride he gave Buck the spare pistol and the box of rifle cartridges.

'I sure hate riding off and leaving you here,' Matt said, tightening his cinch.

'You can't be in two places at once,' Buck returned. 'Go on while you still can.'

Matt turned and lifted his foot to the stirrup. The black tried to pull away from him and he jerked on the reins. He swung into the saddle and was turning the horse to ride in the direction of B Bar when a burst

114

of fire erupted from the gully mouth and heavy reports mingled with the intermittent flashes of several guns.

The black jumped and shuddered – snorted in sudden agony – then went down heavily, dead before it hit the ground. Matt instinctively kicked his feet from the stirrups as the horse fell with threshing legs, unable to do anything but try to avoid being crushed. He thrust against the saddle horn, kicked his feet out of his irons and vacated the saddle but lost his balance and crashed to the ground beside the horse, jarring his right shoulder on the hard ground. He rolled quickly in an effort to lessen the impact and finished up on his face in the grass with slugs ripping and tearing into the ground around him.

The shooting shut down as suddenly as it had begun. Matt pushed himself to his knees to observe. He saw the black hump of his brother crouched nearby and slithered towards him.

'Are you OK, Buck?' he demanded.

'Yeah, they never touched me but they got your bronc. What do you do now?'

'Take the fight to them.' Matt spoke through his clenched teeth. 'Come on, let's go get them.'

He pushed himself to his feet and cocked his pistol. He faced the gully, which was in deep shadow despite the moonlight, and began shooting into it as he moved forward. Buck ranged himself alongside and they advanced at a half-run, shattering the uneasy silence with aimed shots. Answering fire came from the gully, and Matt realized they were at a big disadvantage out in the open. Buck was firing the Winchester from the hip, and went to ground suddenly, his action sending a stab of alarm through Matt.

'Have you been hit, Buck?' he called.

'They'll have to do better than that to nail me,' his brother replied with a harsh laugh. 'Move off to the left a bit and put some space between us. I'll go forward while you shoot, then take over while you catch up. Start shooting, Matt.'

Matt triggered three quick shots. Buck got up and ran forward several yards before dropping into cover and working the rifle. Matt sprang up and raced forward, ignoring the lead that came at him out of the shadows. When he dropped into cover again he emptied the remaining loads in his pistol at the gun flashes emanating from the gully mouth, and was reloading his smoking weapon when Buck started shooting some yards closer to the gully.

They continued to close in, moving and firing alternately, their weapons singing a sullen song of death in the pale moonlight. Matt aimed at gun flashes flaring in the gully and was grimly satisfied when one of the weapons opposing them fell silent. Then the shooting stopped altogether and silence settled over the gully.

'Cover me,' Buck called, and arose and ran forward before Matt could argue about his decision. Matt emptied his pistol into the gully mouth, then sprang up and ran forward, fumbling at his belt for fresh shells. He broke his gun and thumbed cartridges into the cylinder. Buck disappeared into the gully and was swallowed up by the shadows. Two shots sounded and Matt saw the gun flashes. He could smell gunsmoke in the air. He slowed and went to ground, his pistol lifting and ready to trade lead.

'Looks like they've pulled back, Matt.' Buck's harsh voice came floating out of the uncertain darkness. 'Keep your head down when you come in. I heard voices back there by the rustler cave. I think they are getting their horses ready to make a run for it.'

'We need two mounts,' Matt replied, getting to his feet. He went forward recklessly and collided with Buck.

'Keep moving,' Matt urged, and hurried along, stumbling over the rough floor of the gully.

A gun blasted from ahead and the bullet whined through the darkness. Matt ignored it, aware that it had not been aimed directly at them. He caught the gleam of a low fire ahead and quickly sought cover in some rocks. To his right he could hear the restlessness of the herd penned in the grassy area, and guessed the horses of the rustlers would be in with the cattle.

Buck had moved in the direction of the hard and a voice came out of the darkness.

'Cover me, Matt. We've got between them and their mounts. Some horses are in here with the cattle. I'll bring two out.'

Matt swung to face the cave mouth. He could see nothing beyond the faint gleam of the low fire just outside it. There was no movement anywhere and he crouched with his pistol raised, his finger tight against the trigger. Buck was making noise at his back and the sound must have carried into the cave for a harsh voice called raucously from the shadows.

'Someone is taking our horses! Try and head them off!'

Shooting erupted again and two figures emerged from the cave and ran towards Matt's position, illuminated briefly by the gleam of the fire. Matt ignored their shooting and snapped off three quick shots when both men were momentarily silhouetted against the fire. Both broke their stride and fell to the ground. The shooting stopped instantly and an uneasy silence filtered back into the smoky atmosphere as the gun echoes faded.

Buck called from the darkness behind Matt.

'I've got two horses, Matt. Is the shooting over?'

'It is as far as the rustlers are concerned.' Matt got up and paced forward to the two inert bodies crumpled just in front of the camp-fire. Gun in hand, he checked them. Both were dead, mute testament to his accurate shooting. 'Stay where you are, Buck. I've got two of them but Tarmy must be around. I'll have to check the cave.'

'It'll take two of us to do that,' Buck advised and came striding forward with the Winchester levelled. 'Cover the left side and I'll move in along here.'

They went forward, and paused at the cave mouth. The silence was intense now,

119

after the shooting, and Matt heard metallic sounds as Buck checked the mechanism of the Winchester.

Matt raised his voice. 'Tarmy, this is Matt Cameron. You can't get away. If you're in the cave then toss out your gun and come out with your hands up. I've got you dead to rights.'

They waited for a reply and Matt heard only the low moaning of the wind coming through the rocks. Buck moved impatiently.

'We're wasting time,' he said. 'Kimber will be pulling out after that shooting, and he won't stop running until he's in the clear. He ain't about to take a chance that a full-blown posse has caught up with him. Cover me, Matt, and I'll flush out anyone inside the cave.'

As he spoke, Buck turned to the fire and picked up a glowing ember. He held it aloft and strode into the cave. Matt moved along with him, pistol ready, and they both halted when they saw the cave was empty.

'Maybe Tarmy took a slug at the mouth of the gully when we rushed them,' Matt observed. 'But he's small fry, Buck. I can pick him up later. Let's go for the outlaws.'

They moved out of the cave and Buck tossed his burning brand into the fire. They walked along the gully in the direction of the cave the outlaws were using. The fire in the cave mouth had flared up as if someone had dumped a fresh load of kindling upon it. Buck uttered a low cry of disappointment when he looked at the picket line and saw the horses were gone.

'They've pulled out!' he cried. 'They've made a run for it out the back way.'

'I'm satisfied with the way this has turned out so far,' Matt responded. 'You'd better ride with me, Buck. There's no point hanging around here now. Let's get back to those horses and hit the trail to B Bar. There'll be another time to get Kimber and his bunch.'

'The hell you say!' Buck spoke through his clenched teeth. 'I can't let that bunch get away now. I've got to keep on their tails, and I'll follow them into Hell if I have to. You do what you've got to do, Matt, and I'll handle my side of the business.'

'OK.' Matt turned away instantly. 'I can't afford to stand arguing about what we should do. I'm heading for B Bar. Track Kimber if you can. If you don't pick up his trail at dawn then head for town and we'll meet up there later. I want to nail that outlaw you said would be after Ginny in the morning.'

'Now you're talking.' Buck moved out at a run, heading for the penned-up cattle and the horses. 'What about the cattle?' he called.

'They'll be all right here until I can get a posse out to pick them up,' Matt replied. 'There's plenty of grass, and a stream runs through the pasture.'

They passed the rustler cave. Buck located the two saddle horses where he had tethered them. And as he pulled the reins free a pistol blasted from inside the grassy area, its flash momentarily lighting up the uneasy stock. Matt felt the tug of the bullet as it passed through the brim of his Stetson. He dropped to the ground instantly. Buck yelled in shock and began triggering shot after shot into the ambusher's position.

SEVEN

Matt yelled for Buck to hold his fire, and had to repeat the order several times before his brother removed his finger from the trigger of the Winchester. Echoes died slowly and gunsmoke drifted. Steers were bawling plaintively, spooked by the shooting. Matt peered from cover, pistol lifting to cover the shadows.

'Tarmy, come on out and give yourself up,' he called. 'You haven't got a chance.'

A pistol boomed twice from the depths of the makeshift corral and slugs whined over Matt's head. When the echoes had faded Tarmy yelled defiantly.

'If you want me, come and get me, tinhorn. I ain't walking out of here alive.'

'Then show yourself and we'll put you out of your misery,' Buck yelled. 'We aim to please.'

'Take those two horses down the gully, Buck,' Matt said. 'I want to get out of here, but fast. I've got a lot of riding to do.'

'I'm not going with you.' Buck arose from

his cover and grabbed the reins of the two horses.

Tarmy fired instantly and the bullet stuck a rock nearby and whined away into the darkness. Matt returned fire before moving away. He was not interested in wasting time trying to take Tarmy now. He caught up with Buck, who halted and handed him the reins of one of the horses.

'This is where we split up, Matt,' Buck said. 'I'll head through Kimber's cave and out the back way. I can't track him in the dark so I'll ride clear of the back gully and then lie up and wait for daylight. The rest I'll play as it comes. You better be careful when you try to take Jesse Coe in the morning. He's real fast, and he won't surrender without a fight. If you get him then you better head back to town and stand by in case Kimber does show up there with the gang. He's got a one-track mind, and he won't give up the idea of hitting the bank in Buffalo Crossing. So long.'

'See you in town,' Matt responded. 'Take it easy, Buck.'

Buck chuckled and began to lead his horse back up the gully in the direction of the outlaw cave. Matt went down the gully and, as they parted, Tarmy blazed away at them from the cattle pen without success.

Matt led the horse out of the gully and swung into the saddle. The horse fought him for a time, not liking a stranger in his saddle, but Matt curbed him and then peered around to get his bearings. The moonlight was sufficient for his purpose and he set off on the long ride to the B Bar ranch. His ears were singing in protest at the shooting that had occurred and he yawned several times in an attempt to clear them.

He knew this part of the country intimately and had no trouble with his direction. The moon had shifted its position in the sky and was now in the west and angling down to disappear behind a range of hills in the distance. He rode steadily, conserving the stamina of the horse for any emergency that might arise. But he had not travelled many yards when he got an uncanny feeling that he was being followed.

Matt reined in sharply and twisted in the saddle to watch his back trail. He caught the sound of a steel-shod hoof striking rock somewhere back there, but the sound was not repeated, as if the follower suddenly realized that his quarry had halted and had reined in also. Matt drew his pistol. He dismounted and trailed the reins, then walked back along his trail for several yards, listening intently. Again he caught the sound of a hoof on rock, and knew by the sound that the rider at his back had also dismounted.

It could only be Jack Tarmy prowling through the night like a sneaking coyote, Matt thought, and grinned with his teeth clenched, aware that he was running out of time and needed to keep riding at full stretch. He turned back to the horse, swung into the saddle, then set out fast, holstering his gun and concentrating on his riding. After several minutes of hammering recklessly through the shadows he reined in to listen intently, and again caught the click of steel against stone. This time the sounds continued, and he drew his pistol and sat waiting for the anonymous rider to appear.

He caught a faint movement, just a slight changing of shadow patterns, and lifted his gun into the aim. A rider materialized out of the gloom, took shape, and approached slowly. Matt stood in deep shadow, covering the newcomer. When the man drew within earshot, Matt called a challenge.

'Hold it right there. I got you covered. Who are you?'

A gun exploded instantly and the bullet passed Matt's left shoulder with a spiteful whine of displaced air. Matt triggered his Colt, his eyes narrowed against the muzzle flame, and saw the rider jerk under the impact of speeding lead, then pitch sideways to the ground. He sat motionless until the echoes had faded to nothing before dismounting and going back with levelled gun.

He found the rider crumpled against a rock, arms out-flung. Matt kicked aside a discarded pistol and bent over the motionless figure to find a dark patch of blood on his shirt front. He was dead. Matt struck a match and held it close to the immobile features and shock speared through him when he saw the man was not Jack Tarmy. He was looking at the lean, rat-like face of Cal Nugent, an odd job man in Buffalo Crossing who worked mainly in Mike Gibson's bar as a cleaner.

The match went out and Matt sat back on his heels in the darkness, gazing at the pale oval of Nugent's rigid features while vibrant shock coursed through him. What was Nugent doing out here? Where had he come from? He never rode with any posse and seemed to spend all his free time in Gibson's Bar; a man who lived on the fringe of

127

lawlessness and took his opportunities as and when they came.

A boot scraped against a rock somewhere close by and Matt flung himself around and to one side as a gun blasted raucously. A slug struck Matt in the left side with the force of a kicking mule. The gun flash dazzled him and he fell back as pain flashed through his lower chest. He felt as if he had been struck by a bolt of lightning but lifted his gun instinctively. Then a boot came out of the shadows on his left side and kicked him solidly in the temple. The whole of creation seemed to explode into ragged fire – all inside his pounding skull, and he relaxed silently into unconsciousness, relieved by the sudden cessation of pain and awareness.

Matt had no idea where he was or what had happened to him when a stab of pain in the left side of his chest brought him out of that dark limbo. He realized that he was face down across a saddle and the horse carrying him was moving at a canter, the jolting saddle causing him untold agony as he was bounced up and down by the animal's uneven gait. A pulse in his skull pounded sullenly. Pain was spearing through his left side and his left arm and he wondered how badly he had been hurt. When he tried to move his injured arm into a more comfortable position he discovered that his wrists were bound together and he was helpless. He lost consciousness again.

When next he opened his eyes grey daylight had chased away the shadows and Matt found himself lying on hard ground on his back. Sunlight was creeping across the range from the east. He tried to lift up a little in order to check his surroundings but his body was cramped by the tight bonds and he slumped inertly. A movement caught his attention and he looked up to see a man standing over him, a cup in his left hand, his bearded face wearing a grin which showed uneven teeth in a crooked smile. Matt gazed at the man, recognizing the face but unable to put a name to it.

'So you ain't gonna die on me,' the man observed with a snickering laugh. 'For a short time back there I thought you were on the way out, and you'd be no good to me dead. The order was to bring you back alive. The man wants the pleasure of killing you personally so don't die on me. I wouldn't collect a penny if you did.'

'What man?' Matt demanded.

'I can't tell you that! If I did and you got

129

away from me you'd go for him and cut me off from my dough. Don't be impatient, mister. You'll meet him all in good time. Make the most of what you've got left of your life, that's my advice. You don't have long now.'

'I've seen you around Buffalo Crossing,' Matt mused, trying to clear his mind so he could think straight. 'You were with Nugent, huh? And the two of you were paid to grab me for someone else.'

'My name ain't important, but you got hold of the right end of the stick now, mister, so stow the gab. We're heading back to Buffalo Crossing where you will get your come-uppance and I'll pick up my money. You've had a good run. We took up your trail when you left town last night. You sure got in a helluva fight with those outlaws, so I ain't taking any chances with you. Just stay quiet and you'll live long enough to see the town again before I hand you over.'

Matt fell silent, his thoughts tumbling through his mind. Each time he drew breath a sharp pain flashed through his left side. His shirt was stiff with dried blood and he felt gaunt after his experiences of the night. He watched the sun come up over the eastern horizon and groaned aloud when he thought of Ginny leaving the B Bar ranch and getting picked up by Jesse Coe. And where was the Kimber gang now? Would the outlaws go ahead with their planned bank raid in spite of the way it was panning out for them? Buck had seemed to think they would.

'Do you wanta sit your saddle or ride face down?' Matt's captor demanded. 'It's all the same to me. Just don't give me any trouble, that's all.'

'I'll sit the saddle,' Matt replied, and the man dragged him off the ground and boosted him into the saddle of the waiting horse. Matt swayed as his senses reeled, and gripped the barrel of the animal with his knees. Pain rippled through his left side. His left arm was hurting badly just above the elbow, and his hand had lost much of its sensation. 'You've got this rope too tight around my wrists,' he said through clenched teeth.

'So it'll keep you harmless.' The man grinned. 'It doesn't matter what condition you're in when we hit town so long as you're alive. Quit your jawing and we'll get on.'

Matt looked around as they moved on. The desolate range stretched away on all sides, seeming illimitable and uninhabited.

It took him some time to pinpoint their position, and despair filled him when he realized the man was keeping away from frequented trails. They rode without stopping and the day passed interminably; every step his horse took, caused Matt untold agonies.

The pain in Matt's chest grew steadily worse as they continued, aggravated by the jolting of the saddle. He tried to keep his mind off his condition and studied his captor. It came to him eventually that he had seen the man often around town, and then remembered seeing him working in Joe Tilney's lumber yard. A name sprang into prominence in his mind.

'You're Sim Hackett,' Matt said. 'I've got you pegged now. You hang out in Gibson's bar when you're not hauling lumber. So who is paying you to bring me in?'

'Stow the questions,' Hackett replied. 'I got nothing to say to you. We ain't far from town now and I'll soon be rid of you.'

'What are you being paid to hand me over?' Matt persisted.

'If you don't shut your mouth I'll bend the barrel of my shooter over your skull and you'll finish the trip face down,' Hackett threatened.

Matt lapsed into silence. It was possible that he would be spotted riding into town, for he knew the sheriff would have a number of able-bodied men positioned around the main street as a reception committee should the Kimber gang show up. The day passed, night fell, and the torturous ride continued. Matt lost consciousness several times during the night, and he was relieved when streaks of grey began to claw through the blackness overhead. The sun came up, and he wondered what had happened to Ginny. Had Jesse Coe grabbed her the previous day as planned?

It was about the middle of the morning when the buildings of Buffalo Crossing showed in the distance.

Hackett kept to low ground, following the natural undulations of the country, and Matt began to fear that they would reach town unseen. They crossed the river that flowed to the west of the town and Hackett turned south along the east bank as if intending to skirt the town but they ended up beside one of the corrals at Hulk Grayson's slaughter house.

'Say, did Grayson pay you to bring me in?' Matt demanded.

'You've hit the nail on the head.' Hackett

grinned. 'There's no need for it to be a secret any longer. Sure! Hulk got angry because you put two slugs in him. He set Tarmy and Motter to get you but you killed Motter instead. Before Tarmy left town he came to see me and Nugent in Gibson's bar. He told us Hulk would pay good money if we grabbed you and brought you back to face him, so we took the job and here you are.'

'You won't get away with it,' Matt warned.

'What can you do about it?' Hackett guffawed. 'I guess it's worked out good for me. Nugent is dead so I'll get all the dough, and that can't be bad any way you look at it. Now stow the gab and get on. We're going into the slaughterhouse, and you won't make a sound if you know what's good for you.'

Matt looked around as Hackett dragged him out of the saddle. His knees gave way and he staggered. Hackett pulled his pistol, thrust the muzzle under Matt's chin, then guided him around the building to a rear entrance overlooking the river. He produced a key and unlocked the door, and had to support Matt as they entered.

'I got orders to put you in here and leave you so you can't get free,' Hackett mused, pushing Matt to the ground and looking around. 'With Hulk in bed nursing his wounds there's no one around here today so we've got the place to ourselves. I know you're hell on wheels when you get going so I'd better fix you good. It wouldn't do to collect dough from Hulk and then he shows up here to find you've escaped.'

'I need to see Doc Crickmore,' Matt said sharply.

'Are you loco? I ain't getting anybody but Hulk. You better stop that kind of talk, or I'll have to shut your mouth for you.'

Hackett looked around the area where animals were slaughtered. Hulk had suspended a running rail from an overhead beam with roller hooks on it which took the dressed beeves into the storage room next door, and he went back to the entrance.

You stay there,' he told Matt, and snickered as if he had made a joke. 'I won't be a minute so behave yourself until I get back.'

Matt tried his bonds as soon as Hackett went outside but the pain in his left side and arm rendered him immobile. He could not move his left arm at all, and when he looked at his bound wrists he saw that his fingers were swollen and had turned an unhealthy purple colour. There was no feeling in them for his bonds were too tight and had constricted his circulation. He looked around desperately, but Hackett returned before he could even think of escaping, and the man was holding a length of rope.

'I'm gonna put a loop around your chest and haul you up on one of those hooks,' Hackett said. 'You'll swing in here until Hulk can get around to you.'

'Hulk won't be able to get around here for days,' Matt protested. 'You can't leave me hanging that long. I'll be dead before Hulk can show up, and if that happens then he will want his dough back.'

'You'll do for now. I'll see Hulk soon as I leave you here.'

Hackett formed a loop in the rope and slipped it over Matt's head and under his arms, pulling it tight before throwing the other end over a hook on the overhead rail. He hauled on the rope and Matt was dragged upwards until his feet were just clear of the ground. Hackett tied the free end of the rope around Matt's waist, knotting it securely behind his back, and then gave Matt a push that set him swinging.

'That takes care of you.' Hackett grinned and turned to depart.

Matt tried to speak but his weight caused the rope to tighten inexorably around his chest until he could scarcely breathe as he swung at the end of the rope. He watched Hackett leave, heard the man's receding footsteps, and when he tried to get free of the rope he discovered that he was completely helpless. The knots were tied out of reach behind his back, and he could not move his hands.

The silence was complete inside the building and no sounds penetrated from outside. Matt wondered what was happening to Buck. Had his brother picked up the trail of Kimber's gang when daylight came? And had the sheriff organized the men of the town into a defensive force which could prevent the robbers getting into the bank? He recalled that Buck said Kimber planned to hit the bank in the afternoon of today just before closing time. If that occurred then he had a little time to spare, but he could not see how he could escape from this situation without help.

He was unable to record the passage of time and impatience chafed at his mind. He closed his eyes and tried to conserve what little strength he had left. Surprisingly, he drowsed despite his discomfort, and jerked back to full awareness when he heard the back door opening noisily. He lifted his head and saw Sam Beeson, Hulk Grayson's odd job man entering the building.

'Hey, Sam,' he called. 'Come over here and cut me loose.'

Beeson was old, looked to be in his sixties, and had never been bright. He drank a lot and could he trusted to do only the simplest chores. He paused, his slight figure swaying slightly as he looked around the dim interior of the slaughterhouse. When he saw Matt bound and suspended from the rail he half turned towards the door, took a step towards it, then paused and looked again at Matt, his expression evincing a procession of different emotions from shocked surprise to sheer disbelief.

'Come and cut me down, Sam,' Matt repeated.

Sam frowned and shambled across to stand before Matt, the reek of whiskey emanating from him. He shook his head as if he could not believe his eyes. Then he shrugged as if it was all beyond him and wiped his mouth with the back of his hand.

'You're Matt the deputy, ain't you?' Sam

demanded in a hoarse voice. 'What are you doing up there, son?'

'Someone is playing a joke on me,' Matt replied, not wanting to overload Sam's misted brain with details. 'Cut me down, will you?'

'I saw Sim Hackett in Gibson's bar and he told me to leave you hanging. He said you'd been shot and you're on the hook to straighten you out. I can see blood on you. Who did the shooting?'

'Never mind about that, Sam; just do like I ask you. For God's sake cut me down!'

'I can't rightly do that. I only work here, and as Hackett told me to leave you alone it could be more than my job is worth to turn you loose.'

Matt groaned inwardly when Sam turned away and picked up a broom.

'Sam, you were in the army during the war, weren't you?' Matt demanded.

Sam paused and stood to attention. He used the broom as a rifle and went through a series of drill movements, shouting orders to himself as he did so. He turned about and marched the length of the long room, calling out the step, and then returned to confront Matt.

'You never forget the drill no matter how

long it's been since you did it,' he said.

'Were you a good soldier, Sam?'

'I sure was.' Sam straightened again and prepared to go through his drill movements once more.

'Did you always obey orders, Sam?' Matt cut in.

'Sure did.' Sam nodded emphatically. 'Always obey the last order, they said, and you'd get it hot if you didn't do it quick enough.'

'I'm giving you an order, soldier,' Matt shouted, his voice echoing. 'Cut me loose this minute, or else!'

'You can't give me orders, Matt. You ain't in the army and I don't have to do what you say. I got my orders before I came in here and I'll carry them out.'

He returned to his sweeping, and Matt gazed at him in despair, wondering how to penetrate the mist clouding Sam's brain. Then a thought occurred to him and he tried again.

'Sam, you always wanted to be a deputy sheriff, didn't you?' he demanded.

Sam dropped the broom and came to confront Matt, his head nodding eager agreement.

'I'd have made a good lawman, but Tom

Flynn said I was too stupid to be a deputy,'
he said.

'I don't think the sheriff was right. Take
my star off my coat, Sam, and pin it on your
chest. I'll make you a deputy, but hurry it up
before someone comes in here and spoils it
for you.'

Sam's expression changed and his pale
eyes gleamed. He removed Matt's law badge
and pinned it to his shirt.

'Now raise your right hand,' Matt ordered,
and when Sam obeyed Matt swore him in as
a deputy sheriff.

'I took the oath so I'm a deputy now,' Sam
said happily.

'You sure are.' Matt drew a deep breath.
'And you're wearing a badge to prove it. I'm
the chief deputy, Sam and you have to obey
my orders.'

'Sure, but I can't turn you loose, Matt. It
would be more than my job is worth. I got
to do like I've been told.'

Matt was ready to give up but decided to
try another angle in an attempt to prise a
little sense into Sam's mind.

'OK, so don't turn me loose if you think
you shouldn't, Sam. But you could go and
tell Sheriff Flynn that I'm hung up in here.'

'No I can't do that either.' Sam shook his

head. 'Hackett told me to stay away from the law.'

'What about Bella?' Matt demanded in some desperation. 'She's Hulk's wife so you could tell her. Go fetch her, Sam. Tell her it's urgent. I need to talk to her.'

'OK! Why didn't you say so before? Bella's all right. She's been real good to me. I'll go tell her about you.'

Matt drew a deep breath as Sam departed. He waited anxiously for Bella to arrive. He thought she had set him up for Jack Tarmy although she had protested her innocence, and he had no choice but to put her to the test.

Time seemed to stand still as Matt waited, and he had to struggle to maintain his patience. There was so much to be done and yet he felt he would not find the strength or energy to do anything even if he managed to get free of his bonds.

He closed his eyes and tried to relax. Pain coursed through his body with every tortured breath he took. When the back door creaked open he lifted his head and peered towards it, relief swelling inside him. Was it Bella at last? He narrowed his eyes as a figure stepped into the dim interior of the slaughterhouse and came towards him and had trouble focusing his gaze, but saw immediately that it was not Bella. Horror stabbed through him when he recognized Jack Tarmy, who was wearing a wide grin and holding a drawn pistol...

EIGHT

Tarmy grinned when he paused before Matt. He reached out and pushed Matt to set him swinging, and his raucous laughter echoed in the big room.

'I didn't believe Hackett when he told me he'd got you. But you killed Nugent, huh? That was a bad thing to do. I'd like to kill you here and now but Hulk wants that pleasure so I got to leave you to him. He'll be about later today, and you'll be the first man he'll want to see. I'm on my way now to tell him that you're helpless in here, and I hope he'll let me watch you get the chop.'

'I was hoping we'd killed you at the hide-out,' Matt said heavily. 'Whose cattle did you steal this time?'

'You ain't ever gonna find out.' Tarmy pushed Matt again and watched him swinging. 'So long, sucker The sooner I report to Hulk the sooner he'll come down here to finish you off. When I've seen him I'm gonna drop into the law office and turn my pard Grove loose.'

Tarmy departed and Matt heaved a sigh of relief, hoping that Bella and Tarmy would not meet. He listened intently for approaching footsteps but heard nothing. The silence in the slaughterhouse was so intense it hurt his ears, but his optimism was high. With just a little luck he could get out of here.

He was drowsing again when the back door creaked open once more and he lifted his head. Disappointment filled him when he saw Sam entering alone. The old man came to him, pulling a hunting knife out of a sheath on his belt. For a moment Matt feared Sam was going to stab him, but Sam waved the knife.

'Bella ain't coming. I told her about you and she said for me to cut you loose.'

'Then get on with it,' Matt said heavily. 'I need to get out of here, Sam. Cut me free, for God's sake.'

Sam went behind Matt and cut the rope. Matt fell heavily to the ground and landed on his left side. Pain lashed through him and he could not move for several moments. Then Sam cut the rope binding Matt's wrists, and Matt suffered agony when his circulation started moving normally.

'Is there anything else I can do for you?' Sam asked.

'Have you got a gun?'

Sam shook his head. 'No, but I've seen a pistol on the desk in Hulk's office.'

'Thanks, Sam. I'll talk to you again later. Right now I've got to get moving.' Matt tried to get up from the floor but his cramped legs would not support him. He groaned and fell back, striking his left arm again, and sweat beaded his forehead. 'Give me a hand up, Sam,' he said, and the old man came to help.

Matt's senses swam when he finally made it to his feet, and he leaned heavily on Sam, who staggered under his weight.

'You ain't gonna get very far under your own steam,' Sam observed. 'Where do you want to go first?'

'I need to report to the law office. But get Hulk's pistol out of his office. I need a gun in my hand.'

Sam went off and Matt shuffled along behind, swaying and reeling, but feeling easier with each passing moment and, when Sam returned brandishing a gun, Matt took the weapon and checked it. He slid it into his empty holster and straightened his shoulders.

'I think I can make it on my own now, Sam,' he said. 'Thanks for your help.'

Sam turned away and picked up his

broom. Matt staggered to the door and left, almost losing his balance on the steps leading down from the office, but by the time he reached the alley beside the bank he was feeling more in control of himself. The pain in his left side and arm was excruciating but he suffered it gladly, thankful that he had escaped from the slaughterhouse.

He paused on the main street and looked around critically. The town was quiet, with no evidence of possemen on the street, but that did not surprise him because the sheriff would have expected the bank raid on the day before, and when it hadn't happened he would have stood his posse down. Matt looked towards the school house on the edge of town, thinking it looked deserted. Making an effort, he walked unsteadily to the law office, found it locked, and felt in a pocket for his key. He unlocked the door, pushed it open, and almost fell over the inert body of Sheriff Flynn stretched out just inside on the threshold.

Matt bent over the sheriff, thinking the old lawman had collapsed, but there was a bruise on Flynn's forehead from which blood was trickling. Matt looked around the office, saw the door to the cells standing ajar, and drew his pistol as he hurried into the cell block. The back door stood wide open and Zeb Grove was gone from his cell. Matt heaved a regretful sigh. Tarmy had got here first.

Flynn was beginning to stir when Matt went back to him. He helped the sheriff into a seat and fetched some water. Flynn opened his eyes.

'What happened to you?' Matt demanded.

'It was Tarmy! He came busting in here with a gun in his hand and laid the barrel across me before I could grasp what was going on.' Flynn blinked and raised a hand to his head. He uttered a gasp when he saw Matt's bloodstained shirt. 'Say, you look like you've been in a war! Are you bad hurt?'

'I'm OK. Has anything happened around town? It looks quiet enough.'

'Not a thing! We waited all day yesterday but there was no sign of Kimber and his gang so I released the posse last night.'

'You'd better call them out again.' Matt sat on a corner of the desk. He could barely focus on the sheriff's face. 'Kimber is bringing his gang in this afternoon just before closing time at the bank. Can I leave the defence of the town in your hands, Tom? I've got other things to do right now. I want to pick up Tarmy, Grove, and Sim Hackett

149

before I do anything else.' Matt explained some of the incidents which had occurred after he had ridden out with the posse. 'And if Hulk Grayson is well enough to sit in a cell then I'll bring him in,' he added, and then told the sheriff about being taken by Hackett and being strung up in the slaughterhouse. 'My posse should be on its way back here by now,' he concluded, 'and with any luck they'll arrive before Kimber shows up.'

'Frank Wenn came in with his wife after you turned him loose out at his place and told me what happened. Kimber pulled out, and I don't think he'll come back if he thinks Pinkerton has got men around.'

'Don't be too sure of that. Kimber has changed his plans somewhat. I reckon he will show up, and I'm worried about him taking more hostages.'

'Well, Frank Wenn and his wife are safe in town. You better get yourself cleaned up before you do anything else, and visit Doc Crickmore.'

'I feel like I've been stomped by a herd of steers,' Matt admitted ruefully. 'What about you, Tom? You ain't looking too good.'

'I'll be OK while I'm sitting here in the office.' Flynn put a tentative hand to his head. 'That damn Tarmy gave me a head-ache. I'll have something to say to him when you do bring him in.'

Matt suppressed a sigh and forced himself to his feet. He staggered, and was forced to lean on the desk, his head hung over and his eyes closed. When the bad feeling passed he straightened.

'What I really need is a good sleep,' he remarked. 'But that will have to wait.' He leaned his weight forward and his feet moved instinctively to maintain his balance. He crossed to the street door and blundered against it as he dragged it open, hurting his left arm in the process. 'I'd better see Doc now,' he decided, and departed.

The street seemed to undulate, and Matt leaned on a nearby hitch rail and closed his eyes. A buzzing sound filled his ears and he began to fear he would pass out but fought against encroaching weakness and straight-ened. His feet were like lead and, when he lurched forward into motion, his knees felt as if they were hinged and his legs did not belong to him. When he took a few steps he could not tell if he were lifting his feet or putting them down. The sidewalk acted as if it was made of rubber and he seemed to bounce along. There was fire in his injured side and arm which bothered him greatly as he made his uncertain way to Doc Crickmore's house.

A voice called his name from a building as he continued, but he ignored it, afraid that if he stopped he would not get moving again. He reached the doctor's front door and leaned against it, trying to summon up strength to knock, but the door opened unexpectedly and a woman patient emerged. She took one look at Matt's bloodstained shirt and grasped his uninjured arm to help him, her voice shrill as she called for Crickmore.

What followed was hazy in Matt's mind. Crickmore appeared, led him into his office without question, and eased him down on to the examination couch. He cut away Matt's blood-soaked shirt and then bathed the wounds Matt had received. Matt remained silent, his eyes closed, his senses gyrating and receding.

'It isn't as bad as it looked when I first saw you,' Crickmore told him. 'You've lost flesh from your lower rib, which deflected the bullet into your arm. No bones are broken. That's luck for you! I'll dress the wounds and then you'll feel a lot easier.'

Matt bore the treatment stoically. Finally,

Crickmore stood over him and enquired how he felt.

'I'm tired and hungry,' Matt said. 'I didn't get any sleep for two nights, and I can't stop for food right now. I've go to pick up some bad men and that won't wait. How is Hulk Grayson doing? Can he get up and move around yet?'

'You put two slugs in his left shoulder two nights ago,' Crickmore protested. 'Any average man would be on his back for a couple of weeks, but Hulk is breathing fire and brimstone. He wants to get up and kill you, Matt.'

'Is he well enough to sit in a cell?' Matt demanded.

'Sure! And I'll be happy to get him off my hands. I can come into the jail to dress his wounds. He's up in one of my rooms, and he's a damn nuisance, wanting constant attention. I tried to get Bella to come in and nurse him but she doesn't want to know, and told me to keep him here as long as possible.'

'I'll take him off your hands before the day is over,' Matt said. 'Right now I'd better get some food. I'm feeling like all hell at the moment. Thanks for tending me, Doc. Send the bill to the law office.'

'Maybe you should rest up here for a spell,' Crickmore mused. 'The town is quiet. It doesn't look like Kimber is coming in to rob the bank after all.'

'I think he will show later. Anyway, we can't afford to take any chances.' Matt pushed himself up off the couch, took an experimental step towards the door, and was faintly surprised that he was feeling better than when he had arrived. He kept moving and departed, to stand outside the house and draw the pistol he was carrying. He emptied the cylinder of its loads and thumbed fresh shells into the weapon. His steps were unsteady as he walked to the restaurant, and he stumbled drunkenly in through the doorway as his senses whirled.

Rosie, the waitress, was setting up the tables for the noon meal, and she exclaimed in shock when she looked up and saw Matt's bloodstained shirt.

'What in the Lord's name happened to you, Matt?' she demanded.

'I'm OK. Just get me something to eat, Rosie. I'm plumb tuckered out and I'll have to sit down before I fall down.'

He staggered to a corner table and flopped heavily into a chair, then drew his pistol and laid it on the table by his right hand. Rosie hurried into the kitchen, and a moment later Pete Mason, the diner owner, came to Matt's table and gazed at him.

'What are you trying to do, Matt, scare off my customers?' Mason demanded. 'You could at least have put on a clean shirt before coming in to eat.'

'I need food more than a shirt,' Matt replied harshly, 'and I'll be out of here before your diners show up. Don't give me a hard time, Pete. Get me a clean shirt if you're concerned for your diners.'

'I'll get you one of mine.' Mason turned away.

Matt slumped in his seat. Faintness was attacking him in disconcerting waves of increasing weakness and he had to struggle mentally to remain alert. Rosie brought him a plate of hot food and he began to eat, having to force himself to go through the motions. His right hand was trembling almost uncontrollably and, initially, he spilled more food than he managed to put in his mouth but persevered and, as he ate the meal, his empty stomach began to settle. By the time he had finished eating, the faintness had passed and he was beginning to feel normal.

Rosie brought one of Pete Mason's shirts,

helped Matt into it, and fastened the buttons.

'That's better, but you still don't look right,' she said critically. 'What's going on around town? This used to be a real quiet place.'

'It'll quieten down again when I've arrested some bad men who have come out of the woodwork.' Matt lifted his hand to check the trembling he had noticed earlier and a sigh of relief escaped him when he saw the weakness had gone. He reached into a pocket for his money and paid for the meal. 'Thanks, Rosie.'

He was getting to his feet when Bella Grayson emerged from the kitchen, looked around, and uttered an exclamation when she saw him. Matt sat down again as she approached his table. Bella's face was pale; her eyes filled with anxiety.

'Matt, I've got to talk to you,' she said so quickly she stumbled over her words. 'I saw you come in here but I had to get round to the back door because Jack Tarmy is watching the street and I don't want him to see me.'

'You want to set me up again for Tarmy and his pards, is that it?' Matt asked.

'No! That's the last thing I want. I was

156

forced into that business because Tarmy threatened to kill Hulk if I didn't go along with his plot. My hands were tied because I need Hulk free and able to run his business. Anyway, you didn't get hurt and you killed Rube Motter.'

'It'll be a long time before Hulk is free again,' Matt said firmly. 'The fool damn near choked me to death. He's got too fond of beating up everyone who doesn't agree with him, especially where you are concerned, and when he attacked me for no good reason it was time the law did something to straighten him out. He was lucky I didn't shoot him dead, but that isn't the end of it. He's got to be taught a lesson, Bella, and I'm gonna throw the book at him.'

'I'll do a deal with you,' Bella said tensely. 'Let Hulk off and I'll tell you where Tarmy is now and what he's up to.'

'If you've got any information about Tarmy then you should report it to the law with no strings attached,' Matt said severely. 'It's the duty of every law-abiding person to report wrong-doing. So what is Tarmy planning? Whatever it is, he won't get very far because I'm about to go through the town for him.'

'He dropped in at the house a short time

ago and told me he did a deal with Eli Kimber out at the hideout,' Bella said fiercely.

Matt's teeth clicked together as he considered Bella's words, and recalled the incidents that had taken place at the outlaw hideout. Buck had recognized Kimber's voice when the gang boss spoke to Tarmy outside the rustler cave.

'So what is Tarmy gonna do, Bella? Come on, out with it. You know I can't make any deals, but I could go easy on Hulk if you do help me.'

'That's all I ask,' Bella said eagerly. 'Just go easy on Hulk.'

'Consider it done. Now what about Tarmy?'

'Kimber told him to get some men together and cause a diversion around town this afternoon when the outlaws come in to rob the bank, and Tarmy agreed to do it. There are a dozen rustlers he works with when he's got a big cattle steal going, and they're always ready to pick up some money on the side.'

'Where is Tarmy now?' Matt asked. 'It's time I put a stop to his activities. I don't need him siding with Kimber.'

'He went to the jail to bust Grove out.'

'Are you sure about what you're telling me, Bella? It's a serious crime to mislead a lawman.'

'It's the Gospel truth.' Bella placed a hand on her breast.

'OK. What you'd better do right now is go along to the doc's place and stay there with Hulk. Keep clear of the street, and have no more contact with Tarmy.'

'You'll find Tarmy and Grove in Gibson's bar.' Bella heaved a long sigh. 'That's all I can tell you, Matt.'

'It'll be enough, if it is the truth.' Matt got to his feet and picked up his pistol from the table. 'I'll talk to you again later.'

Bella turned and hurried away into the kitchen and Matt followed her to gain the back lots. He waited until Bella had turned into an alley and then headed for the rear of Gibson's bar. He favoured his left arm, holding his hand across his chest with his elbow tucked in against his damaged rib. The pain had lessened since Doc Crickmore had treated him and he kept his right hand down at his side, his fingers close to the butt of the holstered pistol.

The back door to Gibson's bar was locked when Matt tried it, and he paused to consider the situation. He moved into the alley beside the bar and looked through a side window to check the interior. Two men were standing at the bar and Mike Gibson was at his usual place behind it. There was no sign of Tarmy or Grove. Matt shook his head as he considered Bella's information, aware that she could not be trusted. He went along the alley to the street end and eased forward to check his surroundings.

The main street seemed too quiet, Matt thought, and a string of questions filtered through his mind. Would Kimber turn up with his gang? What had happened to Jesse Coe? The outlaw was supposed to have taken Ginny hostage when she left the B Bar ranch for town yesterday morning. Had he done so? And what was Buck doing at this moment? Was he on the trail of the gang? Matt's thoughts were tangled with questions and doubt as he emerged from the alley and walked to the door of Gibson's bar to check for Tarmy and Grove.

One of the two men at the bar turned for the door the instant Matt entered, and departed without a glance at him. Mike Gibson picked up a glass and a cloth and busied himself as Matt approached the bar. He did not look up when Matt spoke to him.

'Have you seen Jack Tarmy around this

morning, Mike? Matt enquired.

Gibson shook his head and turned away to check some bottles at the back of the bar.

'Just pay attention for a moment,' Matt said sharply, 'and give me a straight answer for once. I asked you a simple question.'

'I ain't seen Tarmy,' Gibson replied. 'And you can see he ain't in here.'

'Is anyone in your back room?' Matt persisted.

'No. It ain't open this time of the day. But go take a look if you don't believe me.'

Matt took a step in the direction of the back room but halted when Gibson turned to face him holding a small pistol in his hand which was pointed at Matt's chest.

'If you check out that back room then it's as good as calling me a liar,' Gibson said in a harsh tone. 'I don't know what you want Tarmy for, but I already told you he ain't here so leave it be. You should be out chasing that outlaw gang instead of hanging around town bothering honest folk. I pay my taxes and I have rights in this town, so why do you chase after the wrong people all the time?'

'Are you loco?' Matt demanded. 'Where do you get off threatening me with a gun? You better put it down or you'll find out just what rights you do have around here. Tarmy busted Zeb Grove out of jail a short time ago and I want them, so don't get in my way, Gibson, or you'll find yourself in a cell.'

Gibson gazed at Matt for some moments before lowering the gun.

'Put it down on the bar,' Matt said, and snatched up the weapon when Gibson complied. 'Now we'll both take a look in the back room, just for the record.' Matt waved the gun in Gibson's face. 'And you can lead the way.'

Gibson shrugged and came out from behind the bar. He walked to the door of the back room and Matt followed closely. When Gibson put out his hand to push open the door Matt realized it was not completely closed and, as he became aware of the fact, a hand holding a pistol appeared around the door from inside the room and exploded into action almost in Gibson's face. Matt threw himself aside instinctively as two shots hammered through the brooding silence and hot lead crackled across the bar room.

NINE

Matt landed on his right shoulder with jarring force and quickly aimed the pistol he had taken from Mike Gibson. The door slammed shut as Gibson fell to his knees, then sprawled on to his face and lay still. Matt pushed himself to his feet and lunged at the door, his right foot lifting at the last moment to crash against the woodwork. The door flew inwards. A gun exploded as the door struck whoever was standing behind it, and Matt sidestepped as the door came back under the force of the kick. Zeb Grove was standing against the wall behind the door, and he pitched forward and fell on his face, his gun spilling from his hand. Matt glanced around quickly and was surprised to see the room was otherwise empty: Jack Tarmy was not present.

Grove had accidentally shot himself in the right thigh and lay groaning on the floor, gripping his leg with blood seeping through his fingers. Matt stepped in close and picked up Grove's discarded pistol.

'Where's Tarmy?' Matt demanded.

'Why ask me?' Grove countered through clenched teeth. 'He told me to wait here. I don't know where he's gone. Get me to the doctor before I bleed to death.'

'You're going back into jail.' Matt bent over Grove and searched him for weapons, straightening when he found none. 'Can you walk?' he demanded.

'The hell I can! I'm bleeding to death!'

Matt holstered his pistol, grasped Grove by an arm and dragged him up off the floor, half-supporting him as they left the room. Matt stopped in surprise in the doorway to the bar for Mike Gibson was still lying on the floor where he had fallen and blood was seeping from his chest.

'Hell, you got Gibson with one of your shots,' Matt rapped, and thrust Grove into a nearby seat. He bent over the saloon man and examined him, shaking his head when he found a bullet hole in the centre of Gibson's chest. 'You killed him!' he rasped.

'He asked for it,' Grove retorted. 'He was bringing you into the room. Tarmy said he couldn't be trusted.'

Matt dragged Grove to his feet and propelled him to the street, unmindful of the man's protests at rough treatment. Two men were approaching the bar with drawn guns, attracted by the shooting inside.

'What's going on, Matt?' Charlie Moss was a carpenter who always turned out for the law if required for posse work. 'Hank and me are patrolling the town in case the outlaws show up. Can we do anything?'

'Take Grove to the jail and lock him in. Have you seen anything of Jack Tarmy this morning?'

'Yeah, about half an hour ago,' Hank Halfnight said. 'He was riding out of town and seemed in a real hurry.'

'I also want Sim Hackett,' Matt said.

'Hackett was coming out of the alley beside the bank about an hour ago,' Moss said. 'He went into Brant's Saloon, as I recall.'

'Thanks. I'll pick him up. The town seems real quiet. Have you seen anything unusual this morning?'

'Not a thing, and there are no strangers in town. We've been keeping a close watch, but the rest of the posse have been stood down.'

'When you've locked Grove in a cell you better get the doc to look him over. He shot himself in the leg. Then go around town and get some men organized around the street. I believe Kimber and his bunch will be coming in this afternoon just before the

165

bank closes.'

'The hell you say!' Moss grinned, as he and Halfnight grasped Grove by the arms and escorted him along the sidewalk towards the jail. Matt watched them for a moment before turning to the big saloon, and he eased the pistol in his holster as he pushed through the batwings. The saloon was quiet, with only a few customers, all regulars. Jack Ryder was behind the bar, doing his morning chores, and he straightened and uttered an ejaculation when he saw Matt.

'What happened to you?' he demanded. 'You look like all hell!'

'I'm OK, Jack. Have you seen Sim Hackett his morning?'

'He was in earlier – about an hour ago.' Ryder nodded. 'He didn't stay long. I haven't had many customers this morning. Do you think Kimber will show up today?'

'I believe he will, so nobody can afford to relax. Have you any idea where Hackett went when he left?'

'He had a beer and then took off. I got no idea where he went. Do you want a drink, Matt? You sure look like you need one.

Matt shook his head. 'No thanks. I've got to keep a clear head.'

He went to the batwings and stood there for a moment checking the street. His thoughts were running riot through his mind and he heaved a sigh as he went out to the sidewalk. He noticed a rider coming along the street and waited for the man to reach him, recognizing Frank Welton, one of the B Bar ranch hands. Welton was a tall, slim man in his twenties, and he waved and reined in to the sidewalk when he spotted Matt.

'I'm glad I've seen you, Matt,' Welton said. 'What's going on around here this morning? The town is like a cemetery. I ain't seen a soul yet, except a couple of boys who look like they should be in school. And I noticed when I came by the school that it looked closed up tight.'

'There's been no school for two days,' Matt said. 'We're expecting a visit from the Kimber gang, and we heard they planned to take some school kids as hostages so we closed it.'

'So where is Ginny?' Welton demanded. 'She left the ranch as usual yesterday morning to head for the school, and didn't come home last night.'

'Is that a fact?' Matt demanded in rising alarm.

'I saddled her roan yesterday, like I do

every morning, and watched her ride out on the town trail. Nobody at the ranch got alarmed when she didn't come home last night because she sometimes stops over with Martha Simpson. I came in this morning on an errand, so I'd better have a word with Martha.'

'Did you see anyone hanging around the ranch yesterday when Ginny left?' Matt asked.

Welton shook his head. 'No, and we've been keeping a close watch on the ranch since we lost those steers the other day. Do you think something bad has happened to Ginny?'

'I don't know but I'm sure as hell gonna find out. What are you in town for, Frank?'

'Cookie needs some stuff from the store and I come in once a week to pick up the mail. But I need to find out where Ginny is. What are you gonna do, Matt?'

Matt shook his head. 'I think she was taken as a hostage when she left the ranch yesterday. Fetch my horse for me, Frank. It's in a corral at the slaughterhouse. Bring it along to the law office.'

'Sure, and I'll ride with you. The boss would want me to help you.'

Matt nodded and set off along the street to

the jail. Grove was being put in a cell when he entered, and Sheriff Flynn looked up when Matt burst in on him.

'Where's the fire?' Flynn demanded.

Matt explained and Flynn's face changed expression.

'Heck, you better take a couple of posse-men and head out to B Bar,' Flynn said. 'I should have sent a man out to the ranch two days ago to warn Ginny not to show up for school until further notice. Are you well enough to ride, Matt?'

'I'll do,' Matt replied. 'I'd go through hell and high water if I had to.'

When Frank Welton reined up leading Matt's horse, Matt hastened outside. He tightened his cinch and stepped up into the saddle, grunting as pain stabbed through his left side, but he ignored the discomfort and slipped his feet into the stirrups. He wheeled the horse around to leave town, and set out with a clatter of hoofs with Welton siding him.

They rode fast along the trail to B Bar and the miles slipped by monotonously. Matt was racked by fear, blaming himself for not ensuring that Ginny had been warned of the situation. Two hours of hard riding brought the ranch within sight, and Matt slowed and then halted. He dismounted and checked the trail for sign, looking for the hoofprints of Ginny's favourite horse. Welton reined about and studied the ground from his saddle, and after a few moments he called to Matt.

'Here are tracks that were left by Ginny's roan. I'll ride into the ranch and alert the crew about this while you start following the trail, Matt. I'll bring some help along.'

Matt nodded and walked his horse back to where Welton was standing, checked the tracks and agreed that they had been left by Ginny's horse. He swung into his saddle and set out to follow the prints, which were deep and clear cut in the rain-soaked ground, his keen gaze reading the story of the girl's progress to town. Concern for Ginny's safety flared in his mind.

He saw that Ginny had passed out of sight of the ranch before a fresh set of hoofprints moved in from the left and began to follow her. Matt regarded them with grave suspicion, and a mile along the trail he saw where Ginny had halted, apparently to wait for the unknown rider. The two horses had stood together on the trail before moving off at an angle to the left. Matt did not need too much imagination to deduce that Ginny was riding with the stranger, probably unwillingly.

Matt went on at a canter. The tracks were easy to follow after all the rain of the previous week. He gazed ahead, wondering where Coe was heading. He did not doubt that the outlaw had picked up Ginny as Kimber planned, and now she had been in his rough hands for more than twenty-four hours. His mind reeled when he realized there was so much he did not know about what was happening, and tried desperately to keep his thoughts from dwelling upon Ginny's probable fate.

It soon became apparent that the two sets of tracks were heading towards Jack Tarmy's run-down excuse for a cattle spread. Matt pushed his horse into a faster gait. The position of the sun indicated that the time was around noon, and he guessed the gang would now be moving in on Buffalo Crossing if it was Kimber's intention to hit the bank that afternoon.

When Tarmy's headquarters came into sight Matt did not hesitate. He rode in openly, his right hand close to the butt of his holstered gun. A wisp of smoke was curling up from the tall chimney of the ramshackle cabin but there was no sign of life. He checked the corral, saw no horses, and disappointment filled him when he assumed that Ginny had been taken on from this bleak spot. There was a lean-to near the corral, made of poles, with a roof formed by sods of grass, and a pole had broken causing one corner of the roof to fall in.

Matt crossed the yard, reined in, and stepped down from his saddle.

'Anyone at home?' he called, and his voice echoed eerily as he awaited a reply. He moved to the door of the cabin, certain the place was empty, and was two paces away when the door was jerked open and a man appeared with a drawn gun in his right hand which was levelled at Matt's chest.

'Who in hell are you?' the man demanded belligerently, and Matt's heart seemed to miss a beat as he recognized the outlaw Jesse Coe.

'I'm looking for Jack Tarmy,' Matt said casually.

'Well, he ain't here,' Coe rasped, 'and you're the second man to show up asking for him. I guess he's in town right now, and that's where you'll have to go if you wanta see him. So what happened to you?' Coe was eyeing Matt's left arm, which was held up across the chest.

'My horse threw me yesterday,' Matt replied. A dart of fear stabbed through him when he thought of his star, and then recalled he had given it to Sam Beeson at the slaughterhouse. 'I guess I'll have to head into town.'

He turned to leave, wanting to get away from Coe's deadly gun and, as he walked back to his horse, he heard the rasp of metal against leather as Coe holstered the weapon. Then the cabin door was slammed. He did not look around but climbed into the saddle and rode away with a tingling sensation along his spine as he picked up the trail to town. He rode steadily until he was out of sight of the cabin.

As soon as he was clear, Matt swung off the trail and circled the cabin, staying under cover until he was behind the dilapidated structure. He left his horse in a hollow out of sight of the cabin, walked forward to study the ground for prints, and saw where two horses had been led around from the front of the cabin, their tracks entering a juniper thicket a dozen yards to the right. He walked to the thicket and saw Ginny's roan tethered beside a black horse.

Matt turned instantly to approach the cabin, his right hand resting on the butt of his holstered pistol. He was barely three yards from the back door when he heard hoofbeats out front and ran to the cabin door, which opened to his touch. He heard two shots as he stepped into a small bedroom, gun in hand, and saw Ginny lying hogtied on a bed. She was dishevelled, her face grey with fear, and he raised a finger to his lips, cautioning silence.

The echoes of the shots were fading when the inner door to the bedroom was thrown open and Jesse Coe appeared in the doorway, gun in hand.

'We're getting out of here right now!' Coe said.

He caught sight of Matt and his face changed expression as his pistol lifted. Matt did not have time to talk. He triggered a shot, filling the small room with gun thunder, his muzzle lined up on Coe's chest. The bullet struck the outlaw dead centre and Coe was thrown backwards by the impact. Coe's finger was tightening on his trigger as he took Matt's bullet, and he fired a shot as he went down. The slug crackled past Matt's right ear and went on up through the roof.

Matt bent over Coe. The man was dead. Matt straightened, holstered his pistol, and looked at Ginny, who was struggling against her bonds.

'Hang on a moment, Ginny,' he said. 'Someone arrived out front as I came in. I'd better check it out.'

He stepped over Coe and entered the big front room to cross to the door, and shock hit him hard when he peered outside and saw Frank Welton lying on the ground with his horse standing close by. There was blood on Welton's chest, and Matt could see the cowboy was unconscious. He hurried to Welton's side, dropped to one knee, and was relieved to find that the slug had struck high in the chest and might have missed vital organs.

Welton was breathing heavily, his face pale with shock, his forehead beaded with sweat. Matt spoke to him and Welton's eyes flickered open, unfocused at first, but then realization came to him and his gaze brightened.

'Stay still, Frank.' Matt urged. He opened Welton's dusty shirt to reveal a bullet wound. 'It doesn't look too bad. Ginny is in the cabin, all tied up. I'll cut her loose and we'll get you to town to Doc Crickmore as soon as we can.'

He removed Welton's neckerchief, shook

the dust from it and folded it to make a compress, which he placed over the wound. He pressed Welton's hand to the neckerchief.

'Hold that in place, Frank, and keep it there.'

'Matt,' Welton gasped. 'When I got to the ranch the crew had gone out after rustlers. Cookie told me a herd had been stolen from around Temple Rock. That's why I came back alone.'

'Don't worry about it, Frank. Just hold on until we can get you to the doc.' Matt hurried back into the cabin and released Ginny.

'Are you all right?' he demanded, pulling her up off the bed.

'I am now,' she responded shakily. Tall and slender, she had blonde hair which was tangled, and smudges of dust showed on her lovely face. She was shocked by her experience but her blue eyes were shining with relief. 'I'm so glad to see you, Matt. I feared for my life when that man grabbed me on the trail. It's been like a nightmare. He said he belonged to a gang that is going to rob the bank and I was to be a hostage. How did you find me here?'

'Frank Welton rode into town and told me

you hadn't gone home last night so we back-tracked and picked up your prints. Frank is hurt bad but I think he'll live if we can get him to town fast.'

Ginny gasped at the news and ran out of the cabin to see Welton. Matt followed her closely. Ginny dropped to her knees beside Welton, who was now unconscious, and lifted the compress to check his wound. Her face was grim when she glanced at Matt.

'We've got to get him to Doc Crickmore,' she gasped.

'I noticed a buckboard out back,' Matt replied. 'There should be some harness around, and I'll put two of the horses in the shafts. Stay with Frank, Ginny.'

She nodded and he took Welton's horse with him when he went around the cabin. He checked the lean-to and found harness under the fallen roof, then fetched his horse and harnessed it with Welton's horse to the buckboard. Both horses were uneasy with the situation and began to rear but he quickly brought them under control. He put his and Welton's saddle and gear in the buckboard and then forked in straw before climbing into the driving seat to drive the vehicle around to the front of the cabin.

Welton was still unconscious when they

manhandled him into the buckboard. Matt discovered his left arm was practically useless but Ginny was strong enough to help him swing the wounded man on to the pile of straw.

'You better ride in the buckboard with Frank,' Matt advised. 'I'll fetch your roan and tie it behind. Then we'll get moving. I need to get to town fast. Time is getting away. Kimber's gang is gonna hit the bank later this afternoon.'

'Tarmy was here earlier and I heard him talking with Coe. Kimber doesn't have enough men in the gang to handle the raid so Tarmy is bringing in some of his rustlers to help out.'

'That's what I heard.' Matt's expression was grim. 'We shall see what's going on when we reach town.'

He fetched Ginny's roan and tied it to the back of the buckboard and then climbed into the driving seat. The vehicle moved off and he had to fight the horses for some minutes before they settled down to their unaccustomed role. Then they set off at a fast pace, and Matt watched his surroundings closely as they headed out. He sensed that he would be too late to be in on the defence of the town, and cracked the whip constantly to drive the horses at their best pace.

They had covered about half the distance to Buffalo Crossing when Ginny tapped Matt on the shoulder and shouted in his ear.

'Three riders are coming up behind us,' Ginny said. Her face was pale, her eyes filled with near panic. 'One of them is Jack Tarmy.'

Matt twisted in his seat, spotted the three riders coming along the trail at a gallop, and recognized Tarmy instantly. Another of the trio was Sim Hackett, and Matt clenched his teeth. He wanted both men badly, but not right now.

'Get my rifle, Ginny,' he said.

Ginny turned and dragged the long gun from its saddle scabbard and handed it over.

'Now you better get down in that straw and keep low,' Matt instructed.

'You can't drive the team and take on those three,' Ginny protested. She climbed over the rear of the seat to get beside him and took over the reins. 'Can you handle a rifle with one arm?'

The sound of shooting blasted loudly over the noise of the grating wheels and Matt glanced behind and saw gunsmoke flaring around the three riders. He levered a shell into the breech of the rifle, but his left arm protested painfully as he lifted the weapon to his right shoulder. Slugs crackled around him as he prepared to fight and he soon realized that he could not keep the rifle steady enough to aim properly.

He discarded the rifle, drew his pistol, and pushed Ginny down on the floor in front of the driving seat. She was urging the horses on at their fastest pace. Matt climbed into the back of the buckboard, heedless of the flying lead. He dropped to his knees beside the motionless figure of Frank Welton and prepared to fight. He pushed back his Stetson, wiped beads of sweat from his forehead, and eared back the hammer of his pistol.

Jack Tarmy was spurring his horse, his reins in his left hand. He lifted his Colt .45 and opened fire. Matt ducked as hot lead crackled around him. The shooting was too accurate for comfort, and he knew he could expect no quarter from this trio.

Matt drew a bead on Tarmy, allowed for the speed of the galloping horse and the jolting of the buckboard, and started shooting. He shook his head when Tarmy showed no signs of being hit. It would have been a different matter had he been standing on solid ground, but this kind of fighting was purely luck. He fired two shots in quick succession but still Tarmy came on, and the distance between the three horses and the buckboard rapidly diminished to fifty yards.

A bullet slammed into the side of the buckboard a few inches in front of Matt and he realized that it had come from his left. He threw a glance in that direction and saw two riders out on his flank, galloping in a circle to outflank the buckboard. He lifted his pistol. It was not such a difficult shot to the side. The buckboard and the riders were moving at the same speed. Matt aimed at the nearest horseman, swung his pistol ahead a fraction, and kept the weapon moving as he squeezed the trigger.

The rider was swept from his saddle as if struck by a giant fist. Matt clenched his teeth and sent two shots at the second man, who suddenly lost interest in the fight and wheeled his horse away, swaying in his saddle as he did so. Matt watched until the man fell to the ground before turning his attention to the trio coming up from behind. They were shooting rapidly and hot lead was smacking into the woodwork of the buckboard. Matt ducked instinctively as a near miss snarled in his left ear. He hunkered down and lifted his gun, ready to trade shots, aware that Tarmy was getting much too close for comfort.

At that moment the buckboard collided with a large rock in the trail and the back wheels left the ground before dropping back heavily with a jolt that almost threw Matt out of the vehicle. He flattened himself and held his fire. The buckboard swerved and tilted to the left, and Matt realized that one of the wheels had shattered. Dust flew as the back axle dragged along the uneven trail. Ginny hauled on the reins and gradually brought the vehicle to a halt.

Matt raised himself up, his pistol ready as he prepared to sell his life dearly. He drew a bead on Tarmy and fired as the foresight covered the rustler's chest. Gunsmoke flared from his muzzle. Tarmy pitched sideways out of his saddle and hit the ground hard. His horse came on, but Tarmy lay motionless on his face in the dust. Matt shifted his aim to Hackett. He fired and Hackett jerked upright and reared backwards in his saddle, then pulled on his reins and turned his horse away from the trail.

The third rider came on, shooting wildly, filling the air around Matt with snarling lead. Matt narrowed his eyes and fired deliberately. Gun thunder filled his ears. His gun recoiled, kicking against the heel of his hand. He saw the rider slump forward over his saddle horn before falling sideways to the ground. Matt threw a quick glance at his surroundings and relief filled him. The fight was over.

He stuck the hot muzzle of his pistol between his left elbow and his side, broke the weapon to eject the spent cartridges, and fumbled at his belt to refill the cylinder with fresh shells. His breath was rasping in his throat and the stench of burned powder was sickly in his nostrils. When his gun was reloaded he turned his attention to Frank Welton, who had slid down the buckboard when it tilted, and pulled him into a more comfortable position. Welton was still unconscious.

Matt hauled himself out of the buckboard and looked around for Ginny. He found her still crouched on the floor of the driving seat. She was clutching the reins and holding the two panic-stricken horses under control, her face set in a grim expression, her eyes narrowed and filled with determination.

'Come on out of there, Ginny,' Matt called, and she stirred herself and gazed around. 'Take a look at Frank while I check on those blizzards I shot.'

Ginny nodded and climbed into the buckboard. Matt exhaled deeply to rid his lungs of smoke. He started back along the trail to where Tarmy lay sprawled motionless in the dust, and was checking the rustler when he picked up the sound of many hoofs approaching. He straightened and took a fresh grip on his pistol, looking around quickly to pinpoint the sound, and was shocked to see a dozen riders appearing over a rise off to his right. A gun cracked; the bullet whined over Matt's head, and he drew his pistol, prepared to fight to the death as the newcomers thundered towards him.

TEN

Matt covered the riders and waited for them to draw within effective range. He cuffed away sweat which was running down his forehead and into his eyes, and when he returned his gaze to the riders he recognized the foremost as Gus Redwood, who owned the gun shop in town. Matt lowered his gun and a grin stretched his lips as he wondered what his posse was doing in this area. The riders came up fast, looking travel-worn and tired. They reined in around Matt and Redwood stepped down from his saddle.

'What in hell are you doing out here?' Redwood demanded. 'Your trail disappeared out there by that big rock beyond Antelope Creek where you told us to meet up with you. It was lucky for us we picked up tracks and the trail of a herd of steers going in the right direction from there because it led us right into the hideout. We found some dead men lying around there but no sign of the outlaws. We went right through the cave and into that back gully and found tracks leading out so we followed them.

'There was a rider following the prints of four horses and we tagged along. It took us all yesterday to catch up with them, and we weren't any too soon because the man following the four mounts was holed up in some rocks and those four jaspers had turned on him. They were pouring lead at him when we took a hand and drove them off, and a good thing we did because it was your brother Buck in the rocks. He'd taken a slug and was bleeding bad but we fixed him up and two of the men took him to Spurgeon's ranch to put him in a wagon and drive him to town to see the doc.'

'Is Buck badly hurt?' Matt demanded, struck by a pang of cold fear.

'He wasn't hit in any vitals, but he had lost a lot of blood. I reckon he'll be OK when the doc gets to work on him. He told us you were there earlier and made the outlaws run. That wasn't in the plan, Matt. We had our long ride for nothing.' Redwood glanced around. 'Say it looks like you've been a mite busy. We heard some shooting way off.'

'Frank Welton of B Bar is in the buckboard,' Matt said.

They walked across to the buckboard and

Redwood climbed up beside Welton to examine him. He looked up at Matt and grimaced.

'We better get him to town fast,' he observed. 'Doc Crickmore is sure gonna be busy today.'

'Can I leave you to bring Frank in?' Matt asked. 'I need to get back to town in a hurry. I'm expecting Kimber and his bunch to ride in there any time now to hit the bank.'

'Sure! A couple of us will bring the wagon in. I reckon a rope around that axle and over a saddle horn will hold it off the ground. Take the rest of the posse with you just in case the outlaws show up. But I can't see just four of them riding in while the town is waiting for them. Do you reckon your information is correct?'

'I don't know, but we'd he stupid not to take precautions,' Matt replied.

He borrowed the horse of a posseman who volunteered to ride the rest of the way to town in the buckboard and set out on the trail with Ginny and the rest of the posse. Matt was pensive, his mind filled with thoughts of his brother Buck. When Buffalo Crossing came into sight an hour later he instructed the posse to get off the street quickly and take up positions at points of

187

vantage around the town to await the arrival of the outlaws. He spurred his horse and went on with Ginny at his side.

The town seemed quiet – too quiet, Matt thought as he angled away from the main street to reach the back of the doctor's house. He expected the sheriff had sealed the town off by now and did not want to ride through a gun trap. Ginny stayed at his side, silent and pale-faced, and was at his shoulder when he slid his mount to a halt at Doc Crickmore's back gate and dismounted. She accompanied him around to the front of the house.

Matt hammered on the door and waited impatiently for the doctor to answer. When there was no reply he tried the door and found it locked.

'I'm wondering if Buck has been brought into town yet,' he said as Ginny went to a front window of the doctor's office and peered inside.

'I can see Doc's medical bag inside,' she reported. 'He won't go far without that bag.'

'And Hulk Grayson should be inside,' Matt observed, 'unless the sheriff has been here to arrest Grayson. We'd better get along to the law office, Ginny. I need to find out what's been going on. It's almost closing time at the bank, and Kimber was due to come in just before it closed. The town looks like a ghost town. Come on. Leave the horses out back. We'll pick them up later.'

They walked along the sidewalk towards the law office. Matt saw that the general store was closed, which was unusual, and there was not a single person anywhere on the street. Matt shook his head.

'There should be some men on the street,' he mused, 'otherwise Kimber will smell trouble. I think the sheriff is handling this wrong.'

'There's someone standing in the alley next to the gun shop,' Ginny observed.

Matt narrowed his eyes as he looked across the street. He saw a small male figure moving slightly in the alley mouth, and sunlight glinted on a metal badge on the man's shirt front.

'Heck, that's Sam Beeson,' he said. 'And he's still wearing my deputy badge. What is he doing out here?'

'Why is he wearing your star?' Ginny demanded.

'That's a long story, and I'll tell you about it later. Let's cross the street and tell Sam to get under cover. He hasn't got the sense to go inside if it is raining.'

They crossed the street and walked along the opposite sidewalk. Sam Beeson was still moving around, and Matt frowned when he saw the twin barrels of a shotgun just showing from the alley mouth.

'Drop back, Ginny,' Matt instructed. 'Sam's got a shotgun. I hope that badge on his chest hasn't gone to his head.'

Ginny halted in mid-stride and remained motionless while Matt continued. He moistened his lips and called Beeson's name. The man craned forward to peer at him, and levelled the shotgun around the corner of the alley.

'What are you doing, Sam? What's the shotgun for?'

'Matt, I'm sure glad to see you.' Beeson stepped fully into view and the shotgun barrels lifted skywards. 'I'm watching a stranger who's acting kind of suspicious. He rode into town by the back of the slaughter-house and left his horse in a corral there. I was cleaning out Hulk's office when he came up to the office asking for Hulk. When I told him what had happened he wasn't too pleased. He pulled a knife and threatened to slit my throat if I didn't tell him what was going on, but he let me go when I said I worked for Hulk. He said he'd go along to

190

the doc's place to see Hulk, so I followed him.'

'Where is he now?' Matt asked.

Sam shook his head. 'He knocked at Doc's door and Doc let him in. He stayed about ten minutes, and when he came out he locked the door and put the key in his pocket. I hope he didn't hurt Doc. He stayed off the street, moved along the back lots, and went into the general store by the back way. When he came out I followed him to the rear of Mike's Bar. As far as I know he's still in there, and I'm watching for him to come out.'

'Mike Gibson was killed earlier today,' Matt said. 'His place should be closed. Are you sure the man is still inside?'

'I know what I saw, Matt. He went in and didn't come out.'

'Did he leave by the front door while you were watching out back?'

'Heck, I didn't think of that. I expected him to come out the back door. He's been staying at the rear of all the buildings.'

'You'd better go back to the slaughter-house and get on with your work, Sam,' Matt advised, 'Put that shotgun back where you found it. I'll look into this. And give me back my badge: I need to wear it.'

'You gave me this star,' Beeson lifted a hand to his shirt front, his expression filling with anger. 'I've always wanted to be a deputy, and I ain't about to let you take it back.'

'I'll get you another badge when I've got time,' Matt said. 'Come on, Sam, hand it over. I got a lot to do this afternoon. And you shouldn't be on the street. There's no one else out here, so get under cover and stay there.'

Matt held out his hand for the law star and Beeson removed it reluctantly from his shirt and dropped it into Matt's palm, his face showing disappointment. Matt pinned the badge to his coat, entered the alley, and headed for the back lots. When he glanced back over his shoulder, he saw Sam following him at a distance, the shotgun held ready in his hands, and Ginny was following Beeson.

'Ginny, go to the sheriff's office and stay there until I show,' Matt called.

The girl nodded and hurried away. Matt motioned for Beeson to go and went on. The heavy silence that pervaded the town seemed to have an undertone of menace, and Matt kept his hand close to the butt of his pistol as he made for the rear of Mike's

Bar. He wondered at the identity of the stranger, and was inclined to believe it was one of Kimber's gang – probably Crazy Joe Stott.

Matt reached the back door of Mike's Bar, found it unlocked and drew his pistol as he entered noiselessly. He crossed to an inner door, which stood ajar, and eased it wide to get a look inside the front bar. The door creaked when it was barely half open, sounding loud in the silence – loud enough to attract the attention of the stranger standing at the bar with a bottle of whiskey and a glass before him.

The man whirled to face the door, his right hand dropping to the butt of his holstered gun. He was tall and lean, his Stetson pushed back to reveal a mass of curly blond hair. His features were angular, as if his Maker had chiselled them out of granite, and they wore an habitual expression of merciless intention. His blue eyes were narrowed, wild, gleaming with a strange intensity as Matt stepped forward to reveal his presence with his pistol levelled at the man's big figure.

'Don't pull the gun!' Matt rapped. 'Just what are you doing in here, mister? The place is closed.'

'The back door was unlocked so I came in. I was looking for Mike Gibson.'

'Mike is dead. He was shot.'

'Is that a fact? Well, that's too bad.'

'It is for Mike! And you're Crazy Joe Stott, one of Eli Kimber's gang, aren't you? I recognize your face from a wanted poster out on you. What are you doing in town? And where is Kimber? I heard the gang is coming in this afternoon to rob the bank.'

'You're barking up the wrong tree, mister. I never heard of Kimber and I sure as hell don't ride with a pack of outlaws. What was that name you called me?'

'You are Crazy Joe Stott! You were in town several days ago, when you killed the liveryman, Ben Turner.'

'Not me, mister. Two days ago I was miles from here, and I've never been in this town before. You've got me mixed up with someone else.'

'Get your hands up,' Matt commanded. 'I'm taking you in. If you're not Stott then you've got nothing to worry about. I have a poster on Stott in the law office, and there is a man in town who knows you personally.'

'Who in hell is that? Are you talking about Buck Cameron?'

'Just get your hands up. I'm taking you in.'

Stott raised his hands. Matt stepped around him and slid a big pistol out of the outlaw's tied-down holster.

'Now get moving,' Matt said. 'Out the door and turn left. I guess you know where the law office is. You're in town to look the place over for Kimber, huh?'

Stott shook his head slowly as he gazed at Matt. 'You got a one-track mind, mister,' he observed. 'I keep telling you I ain't the man you take me for.'

'I'll turn you loose if I'm wrong,' Matt told him. 'Get moving.'

Stott shrugged and turned reluctantly. He walked to the front door, found it locked when he tried it and looked questioningly at Matt with a grin on his face.

'We'll leave by the back door,' Matt said. 'Keep your hands high.'

Stott preceded Matt to the back door and, as he stepped out to the back lots, Sam Beeson appeared and jabbed the twin barrels of his shotgun into Stott's side.

'You ain't getting away,' Beeson said angrily. 'I'm a lawman even though I ain't wearing a badge now.'

'Sam, get the hell out of here.' Matt stepped into the doorway behind Stott and thrust his pistol forward as the outlaw turned to his right to face Beeson.

Stott kept moving, and suddenly he was lunging around Beeson, putting the diminutive man between himself and Matt, who cursed and hurled himself forward. Stott got a hand to the shotgun Beeson was holding and tried to snatch it out of Beeson's grasp. Matt reached over Beeson and slammed his pistol barrel against Stott's head. Stott moved to his left, swinging Beeson around to remain behind him. Beeson refused to loose his hold on the shotgun as Stott made a strenuous effort to tear it from his grasp. Matt swung his pistol again, badly handicapped by Beeson. He swiped at Stott again with his pistol barrel and caught him across the left cheek. Blood spurted as Stott yelled in pain.

The outlaw let go of the shotgun with his right hand and threw a punch at Matt over Beeson's head. Beeson was sandwiched between Stott and Matt and finally dragged the twin-barrelled weapon away from Stott. Matt ducked Stott's fist and side-stepped Beeson, trying to get in close. The shotgun exploded almost in Stott's face and a whirling load of buckshot tore into the back wall of Mike's Bar. Stott was not touched by the lethal load of shot and dived away as

Beeson swung the shotgun to let him have the second barrel.

Matt cursed under his breath, handicapped by his left arm and side. He feared Stott would get away and lunged at Beeson with his right shoulder lowered, catching the smaller man full on and sending him crashing against Stott, who was turning to flee. Beeson struck at Stott as he fell against the outlaw and Stott fell with Beeson on top of him. The shotgun discharged its second barrel harmlessly into the air. Matt slammed his pistol barrel against Scott's head as the man tried to scramble to his feet, and struck again with all his strength as Stott whirled to fight. Stott took the blow on his forehead and subsided instantly with a groan. Beeson sprang up, grabbed his shotgun, and raised it to crash the butt against Stott's head.

Matt reached out and thrust the little man away.

'You damn fool, Sam! I told you to get off the street. You're a menace.'

'I was only trying to help, Matt,' Beeson protested.

'Yeah, to help Stott,' Matt rejoined. 'He could have gotten away. Get rid of that shotgun, Sam, and go back to the slaughterhouse. I've had enough of your help.'

Beeson departed and Matt bent over Stott. He searched the man and relieved him of a long-bladed knife which was in a leather sheath on the back of his belt. Matt straightened, shaking his head as he pondered Beeson's attempts to be useful. A movement caught his eye and he turned swiftly to look into the nearby alley mouth. The movement was repeated as Hulk Grayson's massive figure stepped into view.

The town butcher was holding a pistol in his right hand and covered Matt with it. He had a short leather coat over his shoulders but wore no shirt – his left shoulder was swathed in bandages. Hulk's face was grey with shock and he was unsteady on his feet, but his gun did not falter. A lopsided grin appeared on his thick lips when he took in the situation.

'You're still sticking your nose into other people's business, huh?' he bellowed. 'And you got Crazy Joe! I want to kill you myself, Cameron, but it will be better to watch Joe work on you with his knife. I'll enjoy that.' He raised his voice. 'Hey, Joe, wake up and get to work with your blade. There's a deputy here needs trimming down to size.'

'Hulk, stay out of this,' Matt said. 'You're

not that bad in with the law at the moment, so back off.'

'No chance.' Hulk grinned. 'You stuck your nose into my business and plugged me. Well, I've got a finger in Kimber's pie, and have for a long time. It is rich pickings, and with you dead there'll be plenty more gravy coming my way. Tarmy is organizing the rustling, and after this bank raid there will be no holding us. We'll have the world by its tail with a downward pull.'

'Tarmy is dead,' Matt said.

Hulk's laugh rumbled in his massive chest. 'Good try, Cameron, but you ain't man enough to stop Jack Tarmy. He's been running rings around you for months.'

'He's dead now. You better throw down that, gun, Hulk. It's all over as far as you're concerned.'

Matt took a step towards Hulk, who waggled his pistol warningly, but stopped in mid-stride when a small figure emerged from the alley and grasped Hulk's gun hand, pushing it down.

'Hulk, you put that gun away this minute,' Bella cried. 'You promised you wouldn't go after Matt.'

'Get away from me, you crazy bitch!' Hulk jerked his gun hand back up into the aim with such force that Bella was sent flying by the movement. She staggered backwards on her heels and slammed into the wall of Mike's bar. 'Now look what you made me do!' Hulk cursed. 'I told you to stay home and keep outa my hair. I got things to do that won't wait, and giving Cameron his come-uppance is high on the list.'

Hulk half-turned to look at Bella, who had crumpled in the alley, and Matt stepped in. He slammed his Colt against the wrist of Hulk's gun hand and Hulk dropped the weapon as if it had become suddenly hot. Hulk turned angrily, but jolted into immobility when he found himself gazing into the black muzzle of Matt's steady gun.

'Go on,' Matt ground out through his clenched teeth. 'Just give me the chance to plug you again, Hulk. I'd sure like to put a slug through your other shoulder.' He paused and waited for Hulk to move, but the big man heaved a great sigh and slowly raised his right hand in token of surrender.

Matt stepped back well out of reach and glanced at Crazy Joe, who was beginning to stir. There was further movement in the alley and two of his possemen emerged and each stuck a gun against Hulk's massive back.

'Who fired the shotgun?' Doug Redwood asked.

'Take Hulk to the jail,' Matt said. 'I'll bring this one along.' He walked to Crazy Joe's side and stirred the man with the toe of his left foot. 'Come on, you can sleep all you want when you're behind bars. Get to your feet.'

'Matt, Spurgeon's wagon just pulled in along the street,' Redwood said, 'and your brother is in it. The driver said Buck ain't too good. He's being taken to the doc's place.'

'I'll get around to him in a moment,' Matt replied.

Hulk Grayson and Stott were taken to the jail, and Matt heaved a sigh of relief when they had been searched and then locked behind bars. Ginny was seated in a corner and Sheriff Flynn was at his desk. The sheriff listened in silence to Matt's report of the incidents which had taken place out of town.

'You've done well, Matt,' Flynn observed. 'I'll handle this now. You get along to Doc's and see if Buck is OK.' He leaned back in his seat and shook his head. 'I still don't think Kimber will come in here today, but you carry on, Matt. I'll leave the men staked out around the bank until nightfall.'

Matt nodded and departed quickly. He needed to check on Buck. He went to Doc Crickmore's house and found his brother in the doctor's office, being checked over by the doctor. Buck was barely conscious, but he became animated when he saw Matt, and a half-grin came to his lips. His face was ashen and his eyes showed signs of a fever. He had a bullet wound low down in the right side of his chest.

'I wondered how you were doing, Matt,' Buck said in a low tone. 'I guess I made a mess of my side of it. I got careless and Kimber pinned me down. If your posse hadn't showed up when it did I would be dead now. But I heard Kimber talking with Stott just before they jumped me, and they are planning to come in here after dark, snatch the banker from his house, and force him to unlock his safe. You've got to be ready for them, Matt.'

'It's under control, Buck. Don't worry about a thing. We're as ready as we'll ever be.'

Matt saw Buck close his eyes and glanced enquiringly at Doc Crickmore.

'I think he'll pull through Matt,' Crickmore said. 'He'll need a lot of nursing and it will take a long time, but he's got the constitution of an ox. Leave him to me and go get those outlaws. One of them is in town now – Crazy Joe Stott. He came here to see Hulk Grayson, and gave Hulk a gun to hold me here.'

'I've already got Crazy Joe,' Matt said, and departed.

Matt went back to the law office. Flynn was dozing at his desk. Ginny got to her feet, impatience showing in her expression.

'I'm gonna get something to eat,' Matt said. 'How are you fixed? Are you hungry?'

'I'm empty as a drum,' Ginny replied.

'Come on then. I don't expect to get busy until sundown. After we've eaten I'll see you into the hotel. You'd better take a room there for the night.'

Matt escorted Ginny out to the street. He paused and looked around, spotting the position of several of the possemen watching the street. Most of them were up on the roofs of the surrounding buildings. Matt was satisfied the situation was under control and grasped Ginny's arm.

'Come on,' he said. 'We'll go by the back lots. The street is a gun trap for the robbers, and anything could happen if we walk along there.'

They entered the alley beside the jail,

turned left on to the back lots, and walked towards the rear of the diner. Matt kept glancing around, checking his surroundings, his gaze going instinctively to the tall structure of the slaughterhouse by the river behind the bank. Shadows were crawling into the distance. The sun was low on the western horizon. He estimated that it would be full dark in about an hour. He paused, looked around again, and grimaced when he saw Sam Beeson peering out of an alley on the near side of the bank, a shotgun in his hands. Matt heaved a sigh, opened the back door of the restaurant, and stepped aside for Ginny to enter before him. As she crossed the threshold of the building a Colt pistol hammered once with heart-stopping suddenness, and was followed by a shotgun blasting twice in quick succession. Matt jumped as if he had received a load of buckshot.

He drew his pistol, closed the back door of the diner, shutting Ginny inside, and started running in the direction of the disturbance. He could see Sam Beeson lying crumpled in the mouth of the alley, and was three yards from Beeson when a figure emerged from the back yard of the bank and ran towards the slaughterhouse, waving a pistol in his right hand. Matt had paused beside Beeson's motionless figure, and before he had time to draw a breath two more men appeared behind the first, and they were holding bulging gunny sacks.

The bank robbers! How had they got into the bank unseen? Matt lifted his gun, his mind reeling with shock. He recognized the foremost figure as bearded Eli Kimber as the big man swung his pistol to start shooting.

Matt squeezed his trigger. The gun blasted and recoiled and smoke flared in his face. Kimber dropped his gun, dropped to his knees, and pitched on to his face in the mud. Matt cocked his gun as the two men following Kimber began to shoot at him. He dropped to one knee as slugs crackled around him and raised his gun, aiming with deliberation despite his shock at the unexpectedness of the action. He snapped a quick shot at the second man, who fell instantly, dropping his bulging sack, which opened on impact with the ground and spilled wads of greenbacks.

The third man turned desperately to return to the cover of the rear of the bank. Matt fired a warning shot, but the outlaw lifted his pistol, determined to fight to the death. Matt flinched as a slug crackled in his left ear but his shooting was not affected. He fired two shots and the man pitched to the ground, gun and sack falling from his grasp.

The thunderous echoes of the shooting faded slowly across the town. Matt wondered at the doggedness of the criminal mind. He bent over Sam Beeson, who was dead with a bullet in his chest, the shotgun discarded by his side, and shook his head slowly as he removed his law star from his chest and pinned it to Sam's blood-soaked shirt.

'You've more than earned that star, Sam,' he said softly, 'and I'll see it is on your chest when they bury you.'

Townsmen came running out of the alley, all talking and shouting excitedly. It struck Matt then that there was nothing left for him to do except pick up the money and write a report. He holstered his pistol, sighed in relief, and pushed through the gathering throng, ignoring their questions. He walked back to the diner. Ginny was standing in the doorway waiting for him, and all he wanted at that moment was to be alone in her company.

The publishers hope that this book has given you enjoyable reading. Large Print Books are especially designed to be as easy to see and hold as possible. If you wish a complete list of our books please ask at your local library or write directly to:

Dales Large Print Books
Magna House, Long Preston,
Skipton, North Yorkshire.
BD23 4ND

This Large Print Book, for people
who cannot read normal print,
is published under the auspices of

THE ULVERSCROFT FOUNDATION

... we hope you have enjoyed this book.
Please think for a moment about those
who have worse eyesight than you ...
and are unable to even read or enjoy
Large Print without great difficulty.

You can help them by sending a
donation, large or small, to:

**The Ulverscroft Foundation,
1, The Green, Bradgate Road,
Anstey, Leicestershire, LE7 7FU,
England.**
or request a copy of our brochure for
more details.

The Foundation will use all donations
to assist those people who are visually
impaired and need special attention
with medical research, diagnosis
and treatment.

Thank you very much for your help.